SHOTS IN THE DARK

The shots didn't come for a while. And then there were just two of them. Two quick shots and then nothing. As if they were waiting till he got into better range or something.

I went out again. You know how it is when you're that sick. How you fade in and out and have these quick dreams. You wake up and you're not sure if they didn't happen and weren't dreams at all. I was canoeing with Paul. It was on this fast gray river that ran just north of our farm. Water always scared Paul. We had a cousin who drowned. Paul saw him when they pulled him out hours later. I guess he never forgot it.

Then there were two more shots. Forty-fives, they sounded like. Colts. Then came the sounds of the Winchester. That would likely be Krohn responding. Then nothing again.

I wondered how Carmody was doing.

The poor kid. He reminded me of Paul in a way, that same kind of earnest innocence.

And then I started feeling better. That teeter-tottering of strength and weakness that comes from malaria sometimes.

Shouts. Gunfire. Glass breaking, windows probably. More shouts. Darkness.

I forced myself to my feet. . . .

GHOST TOWN

ED GORMAN

BERKLEY BOOKS, NEW YORK

This one is for Don Westlake.

This is a work of fiction. Names, characters, places, and incidents are either the product of the author's imagination or are used fictitiously, and any resemblance to actual persons, living or dead, business establishments, events, or locales is entirely coincidental.

GHOST TOWN

A Berkley Book / published by arrangement with
the author

PRINTING HISTORY
Berkley edition / April 2001

The Penguin Putnam Inc. World Wide Web site address is
http://www.penguinputnam.com

ISBN: 0-425-17927-3

BERKLEY®
Berkley Books are published by The Berkley Publishing Group,
a division of Penguin Putnam Inc.,
375 Hudson Street, New York, New York 10014.
BERKLEY and the "B" design
are trademarks belonging to Penguin Putnam Inc.

PRINTED IN THE UNITED STATES OF AMERICA

10 9 8 7 6 5 4 3 2 1

ONE

SOMEBODY SAID THERE was a murder trial, so what the hell. I spent my first morning in town in the county courthouse.

The jury was having a hell of a time making up its mind about the woman on trial and I didn't blame them. She was pretty in a wan sort of way, and her gentle voice trembled whenever she spoke for any length of time.

I didn't know the woman, and it wasn't even all that interesting a case as cases went. During my five years in prison, I became a pretty fair jailhouse lawyer and I read everything I could on murder trials. This was a pretty familiar one. She was well on her way to becoming an old maid—she was over thirty—when she fell in love with a rich town banker. Both sides agreed that he was in love with her, too.

But what the county attorney argued was that her fiancé'd met a woman about eighty miles away—where he'd been attending a banking convention—and decided to marry her instead. This was when Jenny Rice, the woman on trial, shot him in cold blood. Right after he'd given her the bad news, according to the county attorney.

You see the dilemma for the jury. They pretty obviously liked this woman and didn't really want to convict her but what choice did they have? All the defense attorney could do was drag sympathetic witnesses in front of the court. They made the woman sound as if the Pope was thinking about giving her sainthood.

Not that I paid strict attention to all the witnesses. Part of the time I spent contemplating just how I was going to steal back the fifty thousand dollars in diamonds a man called Jed Wylie had stolen from me—after we'd both taken it from the apartment of a real live duchess on Millionaire's Row in Denver.

We'd had another partner, too—crazy bastard named Frank Stodla. Jed Wylie had worked with me as number two man in a burglary team for six heists before getting caught—or rather, before *I* got caught. The duchess came home unexpectedly and, even more unexpectedly, proved to be a damned good shot with the .45 she kept on hand. She got me in the shoulder blade as I was following Jed out the second-story window. I went to prison. And Stodla had managed to get out the window even before Jed had. Jed took all the diamonds and vanished. It had taken me a year out of prison to locate him.

When the trial was over with for that day, I walked over to a saloon adjacent to a small stone bridge and had a beer with my brother Paul.

It was on that Friday afternoon that I first realized he wasn't looking very well. In fact, he looked downright pale and tired. He was ordinarily a lively and good-looking towheaded kid of twenty-two. He got our mom's looks, a more delicate mien than my own. I bore the marks of the paternal side of the family: pretty good-looking, actually, but in a cruder way. You look at Paul and you can see he could be just about anything from an accountant to a schoolteacher. You look at me and you're immediately on guard. I'm a little too smooth, I suppose, especially after I educated myself in prison. Smooth in a way you don't quite trust. Paul, you'd love to see your daughter engaged to; me, you'd reach for the family shotgun—the double-barreled kind.

He'd come to town six weeks ago to do me a favor. I'd heard rumors that Jed Wylie was in one of three places, this burg being one of them. There were some Indian caves around here that Paul wanted to explore. He planned to be a history teacher and was fascinated with Indians. This had been quite the visit for him. He spent five weeks writing a paper of some kind on the local Indian culture, he found Jed Wylie for me, and he fell in love with a young lady doctor I hadn't met as yet.

"So when am I going to meet this lady doctor you say you want to marry?" I asked.

The kid grinned. "I thought we'd all take a ride this weekend, out to this plot of land Laura and I are thinking of buying."

It was hard for me to believe my kid brother was thinking of getting married. "So is she good-looking?"

A shadow passed over Paul's expression. I couldn't tell if he just didn't feel well or if something was troubling him. "You okay, kid?" I placed a hand on his shoulder. He shrugged it off, not unfriendly-like, just to show he was okay.

"I wrote Uncle Jim," he said, changing the subject. Our uncle raised us after our parents died.

"Good."

"Told him we were doing fine and to give our love to Emma." That had been one of those little odd jokes the dark gods liked to play on us sometimes. Uncle Jim had raised us after our folks died in that boating accident. He'd been married to our aunt Sheila for forty years. And then she died of a heart attack. A year later, he gets married again to a woman named Emma. And two weeks after they set up housekeeping, they find out that Emma has heart disease. And now she's dying on him inch by inch.

Uncle Jim had given up on me a long time ago. When I was sent to prison, he told Paul never to have any more contact with me. So the night I got out, Paul ups and packs his carpetbag and sneaks off to meet me—Uncle Jim knew where he went, of course. Paul had been threatening to write to him. And so he'd finally done it.

"I told him you were a salesman and that everything was going great."

"What kind of salesman?" I asked, sipping my beer.

"Huh?"

"You told him I was a salesman. What'd you tell him I sold?" I noted that Paul hadn't touched his beer yet.

"Oh. I see."

"So what'd you tell him?"

He shrugged. I noticed his forehead had a lacquered look. Sweat. But it was nice and cool in here.

"Nothin'. Just told him you sold stuff."

I shook my head. "First principle of lying: Always use a detail."

"I don't follow."

"Well, if you tell me you threw somethin' in a river, tell me which river it was and what time of day it was. That makes it a lot more believable than just saying you threw it in a river somewhere. You see?"

He grinned. "Yeah. I do."

"So when you wrote Uncle Jim, you should've said I sold patent medicines or corsets or farm machinery. That would've made the lie sound believable."

"Man, you know everything."

"Yeah, That's why I spent four years in prison. Because I know everything." I drained my beer.

I saw him wipe his brow. "You need to lie down again, baby boy," I told him. "You need to stay in bed all day and try to beat this thing."

"I just got a cold is all."

"You still need to stay down."

I'd always been this way about him; protective, I guess. I'd hear a storm and the first thing I'd think of was my baby brother and where he was. And if he was safe. I'd get real panic-stricken, like a parent would. Or somebody would tell me somebody got hurt and the first person I'd think of was my little brother. The funny thing was, he was a pretty quiet, obedient kid, not the kind to take a lot of chances. Not the kind to get in trouble. He'd gone as far as the tenth grade and was well educated. He had only one flaw: He wanted to be me. Or, I guess, *be* like me.

He never saw me for what I am, which is a grifter. To him I was like one of those masked thieves you read about in fiction magazines. They're thieves but you like them anyway because they don't hurt people and they only steal from the rich. A poor guy needs something, they're the first to give it to him. I'm nothing like that at all but that's how my brother sees me.

And then he puked.

Right then, right there. No warning. All over the nice

shiny bar top. There was a splashing sound. And then there was the stench.

"You get him the hell out of here right now," the big Irish barkeep said with a grimace. "I ought to make you clean it up."

"He isn't drunk," I said as I helped Paul up. "He's sick."

The barkeep glanced at Paul's full beer mug. "Well, then he shouldn't be in here. Now you two get the hell out."

I got him back to our hotel room. He was so weak he could barely get his clothes off. He was wearing long johns underneath. It was seventy-some degrees outside.

TWO

THE WESTERN TOWNS I was used to generally had their courthouse squares right in the middle of town. Wisconsin towns seemed to prefer theirs a few blocks away from the center.

Wyatt being a county seat, the courthouse ran to three stories of native stone with a small gold dome and an American flag on the roof. Buggies of every different quality, size, and shape filled the streets surrounding the courthouse.

The business section was four square blocks of buildings running to red brick and sandstone and stucco—not a single false front. The signs on the three saloons were discreet and cops in summer-weight khaki uniforms walked the street with Colts and billies. They were a pleasant lot, helpful, patient, and the western cops I knew would've had them for breakfast.

That was when I saw the buckboard being unloaded.

Across the street from the west side of the courthouse

was a two-story sandstone building that said HOSPITAL above its door.

Three big, dusty men were helping three patients, a man and two women, from the buckboard. Even from here I could see how bad they looked, how shaky and skeletal they were. Two of the men took the opposite arms of one of the women but they only got a few steps before she collapsed. One of the men picked her up and carried her inside the hospital. The other woman, dressed in the scruffy clothes of a farm wife, managed to stay upright with help from the third man.

"It's comin'. I told 'em it was comin', and everybody said 'Krohn, you don't know what in blazes yer a-spoutin' off about.' But damned if'n I don't, mister. Damned if I don't. It's the worst kinda malaria and it's comin' fast."

I turned around to face the speaker. He was a strange-looking old man. Thick glasses and white whiskers on a face wrinkled by age and sourness. And faded clothes that smelled of heat and piss.

"You remember Fallon?" he asked.

"What's Fallon?"

"Town up north."

"Guess I'm not from around here."

"Oh." Then there was a long silence.

Old fart wouldn't be happy till I told him where I hailed from. "Wyoming mostly."

"Oh. No wonder you never heerd of Fallon. Six hundred population and then the malaria hit. Killed nearly three hunnerd and fifty people in a week and a half."

I thought of my kid brother. Feared the worst right off, the way I always had. Then I thought of three things: One was that he most likely just had a cold and flu; two was that malaria wasn't fatal that often; and three was that this old fart would probably take great pleasure in scaring the hell out of me. I didn't want to give him the satisfaction.

"And the same kinda malaria that got 'em all in Fallon ten years ago is here now."

"And why would that be?"

He paused and peered at me from behind his glasses. "You're kind of a smirky bastard."

I shrugged. "I just asked a question."

"Yeah, but it was the *way* you asked it." He nodded down the street. "That there's the library. That little sandstone place with the arched roof. That's where I spend most of my daylight time. And you know what I do when I'm in there? I lookit all them medical magazines. So I know what I'm talking about. Don't think I don't." Then he smiled. He had three small front teeth. That was all. Watching him eat a piece of meat must be a sight. "But I stay healthy all the time and you know why?"

I sighed. "Why?"

He whipped out a pint bottle. The label read DR. HAVER-SHAM'S MIRACLE TONIC. He patted it the way you would pat your favorite dog.

"That does it for you, huh?"

"You damned right it does. This Doc Haversham, he ain't no quack. He studied in Austria."

He returned the bottle to his back pocket and said, "Time I be getting to the library, matter of fact."

And then he was gone.

I was still thinking of my brother as I watched an old man being helped down the street by an old woman, likely his wife. Looked like the same sort of thing the two in the wagon had been suffering from. If only they'd known about Doc Haversham who'd studied in Austria. He could've protected them.

The kid was asleep when I got back to our hotel room. His clothes were soaked and so were the bedclothes. He looked even whiter than he had half an hour ago. By now he should've been married with his own family, not traipsing around with the likes of me. When he got better, I was going to make him go away and get himself a job and a woman and a real life.

I went downstairs and gave the desk clerk some money and told him to have the doc come look at the kid soon as possible.

"You got any idea what's wrong with him?" the clerk said. He was middle-aged and nervous.

I told him how he'd been acting.

"Oh, my Lord."

I beat him to it. "I know what you're thinking. Malaria. But the kid's got the flu is all." I smiled. "He's my younger brother. I helped raise him. I've seen him sick plenty of times. He always gets over it. I'm sure the doc'll have something in his bag that'll do the trick."

The clerk gave me a dubious look. "If you say so, sir."

I walked out to Jed Wylie's place, which turned out to be a small mansion built in the fashion of a manor home. Imposing. Especially sitting behind a black wrought-iron fence with front gates at least ten feet tall and an armed guard toting a sawed-off, leaning against a tree smoking a cigarette. The grounds were perfectly tended.

I walked all the way around the estate, trying to see if the place had any particular vulnerabilities. None that I could see. I kept wondering what he'd done to accumulate this kind of wealth. And power. A small town like this, a manor house like that, the man obviously had power.

I spent a good hour out there, staying out of sight of the

guard. At night, there'd probably be not only a guard but
a dog. Maybe two dogs, just to make things tougher. He
would likely have a safe in the place but it would take some
doing to find it. If it was a wall safe, it would probably be
behind a painting. If it was a regular safe, it would be hidden somewhere. A lot of wealthy folks put their safes in
closets and covered them up with shoes and clothes. They
sure don't make it easy for people like me.

All the way back to town I thought of ways I could get
into Wylie's house. If he had a big party, I could get in as
a workman or a servant. If only he'd be kind enough to
have a big party.

The simplest way was to accost him. It was also the
fastest way back to prison. He'd have influence in this town,
and they weren't likely to believe my story that he'd once
been a jewel thief and a con man.

A noon church bell was just tolling as I reached the main
street. Everything here was neat and tidy and new. Even the
sunlight felt new and smelled fresh. Every once in a while
in prison I had storybook dreams about settling down. I
could smell the fresh whitewash on the clothesline in the
back of the little bungalow where I'd live with my blond
wife and tribe of towheaded kids. But in truth that was what
I wanted for Paul, not myself.

I wouldn't have seen him if he hadn't been doffing his
big white Texas Stetson to a prim lady hurrying past him
on the sidewalk. It took me a moment to realize who he
was. He was bald now and fat and in his cheap three-piece
suit he almost looked respectable. But the hat-doffing con-
firmed it: it was Stodla, all right—the third man in the jewel
robbery. His being in town couldn't be a coincidence. I wondered what the hell he was doing here.

The hat-doffing was pure Stodla, a mixture of graciousness and contempt, the way he did everything. He was a crazy bastard. He was one of those people I felt sorry for, but who scared the hell out of me nonetheless. His old man was crazy and kept him chained in a root cellar when he was a little kid. You could still see the scars on his back and shoulders and neck where he'd been beaten. You'd just start to hate the sonofabitch when he'd start crying on you. You never knew when it would start and it never seemed to be for any reason in particular. He'd just start wailing, this big mean guy, and pounding his head against hard stone walls He was in the kind of pain you can't explain to anybody; the kind that just overtakes you and takes a little piece of your life every time you go through it. Love can do it to you, and hate; and so can memory, if you've got Stodla's memories, anyway.

When the woman had passed him, he laid a big green goober on the sidewalk, the pure contempt coming through. Then he went back to talking to the men on the front porch of the saloon.

Things had changed suddenly, with Stodla in town. I didn't know how and I didn't know why. But they had.

I went into the hotel, bought myself a cigar, and entered the small, attached bar for a beer. I had two. I was sorting through what Stodla meant to this whole operation I'd planned. I guess I figured that anybody as troubled as Stodla—he'd once torched a small hotel and was disappointed when nobody died. Not only did he not regret what he did, he joked about them the way other men would joke about fishing or work. I guess I'd just figured that somebody would've killed him by now.

I went upstairs.

I heard voices on the other side of my hotel room door. I knocked and a very slender, dark-haired woman in what they call Gibson Girl attire—the long skirt, frilly high-collared blouse, and hair pulled back in a loose French roll—answered the door. She was delicate and lovely and I wondered who the hell she was and what the hell she was doing with my sick kid brother.

"Yes?" she said.

"Yes yourself," I said. "Who the hell are you?"

"And may I ask you the same?"

"He's my brother, Laura," Paul said weakly from the bed. "Sometimes he can be a royal pain."

"You're sure it's only sometimes?" She looked doubtful as she opened the door wider so I could come inside.

THREE

"HE WAS FALLING asleep," she said, fixing me with an accusing look. "And then you pound on the door and wake him up."

"It's my room, too, you know." I sounded like a little boy she was scolding. I was a little embarrassed that it hadn't occurred to me that this was Paul's fiancée.

"It shouldn't be."

"And why the hell not?"

"Because he has malaria."

I'd been so caught up in her I hadn't really looked at Paul. He looked young and he looked scared as hell. "Laura said it don't mean I'm gonna die, Bryce."

"Of course you're not going to die, kid," I said. Then I looked back at her. Her face was a beautiful impersonal mask that told me nothing. I put out my hand. "I guess I was a little sharp with you."

"Same here," she said. And we shook hands. "I'm Laura Westcott, Paul's fiancée. I'm sorry for the way we had to

meet. I've been working around the clock without sleep."
She smiled with a quick radiance—that smile was sharp as
a dagger. "In fact, I need to get back there now."

I was going to say something to Paul but when I glanced
at him again, I saw that his eyes were closed. The dark
rings around his eyes were even darker. His whole body
was trembling. It scared me to see him this way.

She put a finger to her lips. She then proceeded on tiptoes, and put all her supplies back into her gladstone bag
as quietly as possible.

I followed her out the door and into the hallway. We
were both walking on tiptoes and once she stumbled and
bumped into me. It was cute and we smiled at each other.
It was like being little kids or something.

And then I felt bad. Paul had malaria and I was flirting
with his fiancée. Some older brother I was.

We didn't really talk until we got down to the lobby.

"You've certainly got an admirer there, Mr. Lamont. In
your brother, I mean. Even as sick as he is, he told me all
about how you raised him and took care of him and how
much he admires you."

"Just how sick is he?"

Her lips pinched and for just a moment, she looked away.
Then she said quietly, "Why don't you walk me outside?"

Once we were out in the street, she said, "There are three
types of malaria. The first two types are common in the
Midwest and the West and they're rarely fatal."

"And the third type?"

"I've never experienced it myself. But it generally comes
after a very rainy spring when a lot of land gets turned into
heavy swamps in the low-lying region. And this is a low-
lying region."

"What kind of malaria does Paul have?"

Her eyes met mine. "I don't know yet. Whatever it is, he's not alone. The hospital's almost filled up. It was practically empty forty-eight hours ago."

"He could die?"

She shook her head. "I believe in medicine, Mr. Lamont. Not fortune-telling. There's just too much guessing involved. Right now he seems to be doing about as expected. If his fever has peaked, then he's probably going to be all right. Meaning he may have symptoms the rest of his life but it won't kill him." She paused before adding, "I'm very lucky to have found your brother, Mr. Lamont. I don't want to lose him now." Her pretty face looked pinched at the thought.

"He's lucky to have found you, I think."

"And I'm going to help him every way I can."

"I appreciate that."

"And I'm sorry if you and I got off to a rocky start. This isn't how Paul wanted us to meet."

There were three hotels and two boardinghouses in town. Stodla wasn't staying in any of them. There were also five saloons. He wasn't drinking in any of them at the moment, either.

I was sitting in the park after making all my inquiries. I'd checked in on Paul. He was still sleeping. I took a room down the hall from him. I suppose I should have been worried about catching the fever. But for some reason, sickness usually left me alone. Paul had suffered every infirmity known to kids growing up. I'd suffered through only a few.

My friend with the magic elixir wandered over. Without being asked—not particularly liking him, I wouldn't have asked—he sat down next to me on the park bench and declared, "I hear your kid brother's got the stuff, huh?"

"He's going to be fine."

"That's how it started in Fallon. 'Aw, hell, he'll be fine.' Or she'll be fine. Or they'll be fine. Not the kind of malaria you really have to worry about, they said. And then everybody started dying."

I crossed my arms defensively or maybe to prevent them from punching an old man with three teeth. "You sure know how to make people feel better."

"Just tryin' to present you with the facts is all. You could do with some of ole Doc Haversham and so could your brother." And with that he whipped open his vest and dug out an unopened pint of the elixir.

I laughed. "You *sell* this stuff?"

"You damn betcha. I sell it, drink it, bathe in it, and swear by it. Every twelve bottles I sell, the company sends me two bucks and a pack of smokin' tobacco or chewin' tobacco."

"You should've been a preacher."

"Fact is, I started to be but then the war came along and my whole life kinda changed."

"Blue or gray?"

"None o' your damned business."

"Gray," I said. "Otherwise you'd tell me."

"We'd had some damned good men."

"So did we. One of them was my father." I paused, then asked, "What the hell's your name, anyway?"

"Krohn."

"That your first name or last?"

"It make a difference?"

"Not to me, it doesn't," I said. Then, "You're an owly old bastard. You got a cob shoved up your ass or somethin'?"

He giggled. It wasn't a laugh or a snicker or a chuckle. It was a giggle. "I like irritatin' people."

"Well, you do a damned good job of it."

"I take that as a compliment."

I smiled at him. "And that's just the way I meant it."

So we sat there awhile and he said, "I seen you with that doc. She could break your heart."

"She sure could."

"Every young buck in town's after her."

"I'll bet they are."

"I always wanted a gal like that. That looked like that. That had the kind of breeding. You know what I mean."

"Never found her, huh?" I said.

"Oh, I found her all right. I found her ten, twenty times in fact." The giggle again. "It's just they'd never want no part of me. I guess that's why I never got hitched."

We sat some more.

"You give me a gold dollar, I'll tell you somethin' you need to know."

"Yeah? And what would that be?"

"Only way you're gonna find out is to give me that gold dollar."

"You're some kind of human being."

The giggle. "Yeah, and that's just the way I like it."

I dug in my pocket and took out a gold dollar. And flipped it in the air. "Heads, I give it to you. Tails, I decide you're bullshitting me and I keep it for myself."

"Up to you. But I'd sure want to know this piece of information if I was you."

Heads up, it landed. I flipped it over to him and he caught it expertly. He'd probably had a lot of practice.

"You're being followed."

"I am?"

"You bet you are. Don't turn around and look but kind of glance to your left and you'll see the apothecary. In the front window there's a man. He's been following you since you left the hotel."

"How do you know that?"

" 'Cause I was walkin' by the hotel when you left there and I seen this guy watchin' you. So I followed him while he was followin' you."

I caught him first glance, there in the window. Stodla.

"You know him?"

"Yeah," I said.

"He mean you harm?"

"Maybe. Probably. Where's he staying?" I asked.

"Was stayin' in the hotel till about two weeks ago."

"Where's he staying now?"

"Ain't sure." Then, "So was that worth a gold dollar?"

"It sure was."

"I get any other information like that, you want me to bring it to you?"

"Sell it to me, you mean?"

Krohn shrugged and grinned. "I gotta eat, don't I?"

I smiled. "Just as long as I don't have to buy any of that crap you guzzle."

He shook his head. "Some day old Doc Haversham'll be recognized for the genius he is."

"Yeah, him and President Polk." I stood up. "Talk to you soon, Krohn."

I spent the next hour walking around town, peering in shop windows, taking sudden lefts, sudden rights, speeding up, slowing down, just generally having fun with Stodla, who, in his plodding way, kept right after me.

Some of the time I thought about Paul. Some of the time I thought about Jed.

Then I decided to put the double whammy on Stodla. I ducked into an alley and hid in a garage. He came lumbering into the alley, out of breath from hurrying, a few minutes later. He glanced around frantically. No sign of me. He scratched his head, his balls, his ass, and then his head again. It almost looked like a ritual, like making a sign of the cross.

He looked just as big and mean and sluggish as he had when he was still torching buildings in Denver.

He spent ten minutes traipsing up and down the alley. Finally, he gave up. Or so he thought.

He left the alley. I waited five minutes, just in case.

Then *I* started following *him*.

FOUR

IT WAS A nice, respectable two-story white frame house and I wondered what the hell Stodla had to do with it. There was a trellis in the back yard, and a plump woman in a sunbonnet was working in a small garden on her haunches with a lazy cocker spaniel lying in the grass by the side door of the place.

Stodla was a man of saloons and whorehouses and barns with cockfights and ratting going on. He didn't belong here.

The sweet-faced cocker growled at him when he walked past and the woman gardening in the back yard glanced up to see him go to the back door.

"Hello, Mrs. Grayson," he called out, doffing his hat in his theatrical way.

She glowered at him. "I'd appreciate it if you'd leave our brandy alone. Our agreement was that you'd stay in your room and not wander around our house."

"I only took your brandy because I ran out of whiskey."

"That's no excuse."

That cold crazy grin of his. "You know, a lot of people, they're kind of afraid of me, Mrs. Grayson. But I don't guess you're one of them, eh?"

"I don't guess I am," she said, turning away and going back to work with her trowel.

He went inside.

I waited until he'd been inside a few minutes and then I wandered over. The cocker just watched me. Didn't growl.

"Afternoon, ma'am."

"Yes?" She wasn't cold but she wasn't warm either. I got the sense she might still be angry about Stodla.

"I just saw somebody I think I recognize go into your house. That wouldn't be a Mr. Frank Stodla, would it?"

"I should have known," she said. She had a nice, slightly bland face that apparently soured whenever Stodla was discussed. "You're a friend of his."

"More like an acquaintance, I guess. He's rooming with you, is he?"

I guess both of us sensed it at the same time. Stodla behind the curtains in his room, watching us.

I decided to really irritate him. I looked up, waved, and smiled.

She stood up, knees cracking. She dusted damp black earth off of her cotton gloves. "We have an agreement, mister. He can't have no visitors."

"You sure don't seem to like him much."

She raised her eyes to the window where Stodla stood. "I've been told not to say anything about Mr. Stodla." She wiped her hand with the back of her wrist and blew upwards on a piece of gray hair that had fallen over her forehead.

"Now, who would tell you a thing like that?"

She studied me. "Just who are you?"

"A friend of his."

"No, you're not. He just gave me the signal to get rid of you."

"Well, I guess we were friends a long time ago. I guess that'd be a better way of putting it."

"I don't want any trouble with him. Or you. So I'll ask you to kindly get off my land here."

"You're scared, aren't you?"

Her expression hardened. "What I am is none of your concern."

"I'd like to talk to you, all right?"

She glanced back up at Stodla's window. "He just gave me the signal again. Now you get away from me. You hear?" She turned and headed into the house.

I wandered away without looking up at Stodla. She really had been scared. Why would a woman let a room to a man she didn't want to? Who was she, anyway, and what did she have to do with Stodla?

I wanted to ask Krohn about the woman but I couldn't find him. I went up to Paul's room to see how he was doing.

He was awake, lying there. He wasn't pale and sweating like before.

"You got everything you need?" I asked.

"I could do with a couple more magazines, I guess."

"I'll go get you some."

I pulled up a chair and sat down over by the bureau. No sense sitting right on top of him, the germs and all.

"You look a little better."

He grinned. There was so much energy in it that it was shocking. "It was that doc. I think she's got what they call healing hands. She's coming back tonight. I want to get shaved and all before she does."

"Hell, kid, you're sick."

"I just want to look good is all. What the hell you gettin' so cranky about?"

"Oh, nothin', I guess." I stood up and stretched. "Guess I'll go get you those magazines. Any special ones?"

"Short stories. Those are my favorites."

I still felt like hell. Not about my little brother being sweet on the doc, but about me not liking it. "I'll get you some smelly stuff."

His expression brightened. "Hey, really? That's a great idea."

"Time I get done with you, you'll smell prettier than she does."

He grinned, but now it was a tired grin. Even our little exchange here had wasted him again.

"Maybe I'll fall asleep."

"Good idea. I'm going to do a few other things anyway. Then I'll be back."

Usually, the little brother, he'd be all questions. He didn't care. He was too sick to care and now he was using all his spare brain power on that pretty doctor.

I bought a pint of rye and headed to the newspaper office. The press was right in back so when I walked in, it stank pleasantly of ink and paper. The walls were covered with yellowed past front pages and a couple of plaques and awards. There was a counter where you placed ads and paid bills. The only person in the long, narrow place was a pressman in the back. It was about lunchtime and he was washing his hands of ink. A sack lunch sat on a small table stacked with broadsheets.

He saw me and came to the front, drying his hands on a rough towel. "Help you?"

"I'd like to speak with the editor."

"You're speaking to him. Rolfe Dobbs." Then, "Editor and pressman and paper carrier if one of the paper route kids gets sick."

"Wondered if I could talk to you."

He came forward. "Depends on what it is."

"The trial going on. Jenny Rice."

"What about her?" With his glasses halfway down his long nose and his gnarled hands now wrapped around a broom handle, he looked like a Maine farmer.

"Just like some background. I'm a freelance journalist." It was my standard story.

He stopped and studied me, his eyes narrowing in thought. "Ya are, eh? Who you work for?"

"Like I said, I'm freelance."

"Yeah, but a freelancer has to sell his stuff to somebody. And who would that be?"

I reached in my suit jacket and pulled out the pint of rye and put it on the desk. "This is who I work for." If there was a newspaperman somewhere who'd turn down a drink, they kept him well hidden.

He smiled over his pair of store-boughts. "You gonna ply me with that?"

I smiled right back. "I'm sure gonna try,"

"Well, you picked a good time. Just closin' up for lunch. Lemme pull that shade down on the front door and we'll imbibe a little."

Jenny Rice, at least according to him, was going to be set free by this time tomorrow. The reason being that even though everybody knew she'd killed Donald Wylie, they didn't blame her.

"The only bad thing that girl ever did in her life," Dobbs told me.

"Well, but that's a pretty *big* bad thing, don't you think? Killing somebody?"

"He shouldn't have done it."

"Maybe not. But still . . ."

He pointed to the bottle. "I figure I could handle one more shot. That a notion you'd entertain?"

"Entertain and vote in favor of."

He took a pull on the pint, made a face, and set the bottle back on the table. We sat in a small nook in the back of the shop. The back door was open and there was one of those breezes that remind you of when you were a little kid, that scent and that texture on your skin.

"How'd Jed and Donald get along?"

He gave me the judicial eye. "Who the hell are you?"

"You drink my booze and now you turn on me, huh?"

"You're no journalist, freelance or otherwise."

"I'm not, huh?"

"You don't ask the right kind of questions. You just want to know a couple of things and you keep dragging Jed into it when Jed doesn't have anything to do with it."

"You sure you can only handle two drinks?"

"You say a prayer for me if I try and stretch my limit to three?"

"You bet I will."

Dobbs took another pull. "You really want to know about Jed, don't you?"

I shrugged. "Maybe."

"Boy, I got to lay off that booze of yours. I'm startin' to feel it. Can't have town ladies comin' in here and me crocked out of my mind." He shook his head, as if that would clear it. "Jed Wylie. Now there's a subject to make just about anybody sick to his stomach."

"Oh, and why would that be?"

It was the usual litany of offenses compiled by any rich, spoiled, tough, good-looking kid in a respectable small Midwestern town. Too many fights, too many girls, too many instances where the father had had to call in a favor to keep the son out of jail. There'd been a botched abortion, the beating of an old Indian, and the desecration of a Catholic church. Dobbs allowed as how he didn't much care for Catholics—he'd grown up a Methodist in a French-Canuck community upriver and they hadn't been very pleasant to be around—but still and all, defiling a church went against his grain.

As for the Wylie family, Donald, the younger brother, was the serious, studious one. Went to Dartmouth and got his degree in business. Could've stayed east and made himself a fortune but he'd always had his eye on the Rice girl so he came back here and took over the bank operations from his ailing father, And started courting the Rice girl, who, it was said, was lovely to everybody but the colored man who worked for her. Everybody said what handsome kids Donald Wylie and Jenny Rice would have.

Jed, on the other hand, came into a small inheritance when he was twenty-one and used it to roam the country. Nobody ever knew what he did for those seven years. I could've filled in the blanks. Jed returned here when his old man was dying. He obviously didn't expect to be president of the bank but he was pleased when his brother—forgiving all the ways Jed had besmirched the family name in his younger days—made Jed one of two vice presidents.

Jed surprised everybody by settling down and learning

all about banking. Having a lot more natural charm than
his brother, he was handed the most difficult accounts. The
old ladies loved his dash and the crusty old rich men loved
his ruthlessness. Somebody once said that Jed would fore-
close on Jesus Christ himself. He became a respectable part
of a respectable community. He even married a respectable
lady, a woman from two counties over. Her dowry had been
nine hundred acres of prime Wisconsin farmland plus two
hundred head of dairy cattle. They had two children, Jed
became a deacon of his church, and a lot of people in the
Republican Party were saying he should run for governor
sometime here around the turn of the century. He certainly
looked like good material.

"You know a man named Stodla?"

"Met him once," Dobbs said.

"What's he do here?"

"Odd jobs for Jed."

"What kind of odd jobs?"

He shrugged. "Some handyman work. Goes out and looks
over farms or dairy operations the bank might be interested
in buying. He was painting an old building the bank owns
last time I saw him."

"You know a woman named Grayson?"

"Oh, sure. In my day, she was prime material. Broke a
lot of hearts."

I tried squaring that with the woman I'd seen gardening.
I couldn't. "Stodla lives there."

"So I hear."

"She doesn't seem to like it," I said.

"Oh?"

"I asked her about it and she said she was told not to
talk about it. Know what that's all about?"

Dobbs scratched his head. "Guess I don't. Her old man works for Jed at the bank."

A connection was made. I had no idea what it meant. But I would have bet that it meant something. "I see."

He looked up at the wall clock. "I better be finishing up my lunch and getting ready for customers."

"You get a lot of walk-ins?"

"Classifieds, mostly. The retail ads I always got to put on my collar and go out and solicit myself. You'd think after all these years, they'd bring the ads in to me. But nope. They still expect me to go out and sell them myself. Even if they're on contract."

I shook his hand. "You want one more pull?"

"I'd like to. But I'd better not."

I smiled. "I admire your wisdom."

"Ain't wisdom. It's bein' a chickenshit. Town like this, it gets around you drink during the day, you can just about hang it up."

I was just leaving the newspaper office, setting my feet on the sidewalk, when a slight man fell into step with me and said, "I envy you."

"Oh? And why would that be?"

"You're getting to spend time with some of our finest citizens. Mrs. Grayson. Dr. Westcott. Rolfe Dobbs. He's some character, isn't he?"

"I take it you're the law."

"I am. But how could you tell?"

He wore a good brown three-piece suit with a clean celluloid collar and a string tie. He was balding, had a crisp smart little face, and wore nothing that identified him as an officer of the law. He didn't even carry a weapon. Not that I could see anyway. Still and all, he was the law.

"Somebody pointed you out," I said.

"You had to think about that one. Meaning nobody pointed me out. Meaning you've got a nose for law. Meaning you've probably done time somewhere in this great country of ours." He didn't look at me as he spoke. Kept his green eyes straight ahead.

We walked down Main Street together. Just about everybody said hello. Instead of doffing his tan, flat-brimmed hat, he just gave a little salute, touching the brim with two fingers.

"You have business here?" he asked.

"Just looking up an old friend."

"Mind telling me who that'd be, Mr. Lamont?"

"Jed Wylie."

"Well, now," he said, "Jed Wylie. I have to say, you surprised me with that one."

"Any reason I shouldn't be friends with Jed Wylie?"

"Well, let's just say you don't seem to have much in common, you and Jed. You own a bank, Mr. Lamont?"

"Not the last time I looked."

"You a deacon of a church somewhere, are you?"

"No, I'm afraid I'm not."

"You have two sweet little children and a loving, upstanding wife stashed somewhere?"

"I sure wish the answer to that was yes."

"Well, then, you see my point. Its kinda funny that a man like you and a man like him would be friends. No offense."

"None taken."

"In fact, maybe Jed doesn't even *know* that you're friends."

"You could always ask him."

"Now that's a smart idea, Mr. Lamont. Asking him. As a matter of fact, I'm going to see him tonight. For dinner."

He touched one curled end of his mustache with great delicacy. "Turns out he's my brother-in-law and we have a family dinner every Wednesday night."

He gave me that little two-fingered salute. "You take care of yourself, Mr. Lamont."

And then he was gone.

FIVE

I ASKED FOR Jed as soon as I got inside the bank but the thin lady behind the counter told me he was in the next county appraising land, and perhaps there was some way *she* could help me. I said yes, I'd like to speak to Mr. Grayson. And she said, Of course, if I would just follow her to the rear of the bank.

It wasn't a large place but it was carefully appointed with mahogany trim everywhere, and decent imitations of Remington originals hung in gold frames. The staff had obviously been trained to smile at every customer who walked by. This went for men and women alike.

Grayson turned out to be a scrawny, fiftyish man with gray hair, jowls, and a real problem with blinking. His eyelids opened and closed with the silent fury of a hummingbird's wings preparing for flight. I wanted to tack his eyes open.

"Walter, this is Mr. Lamont. Walter is our chief vice president."

He stood up, banging against his desk as he did so. The shoulders of his suitcoat had so much dandruff on them, they looked like snowy mountain peaks. He put his hand out. He had a stunning hard grip, blinking eyes, and dandruff and all.

"I'll leave you gentlemen alone," the woman said.

"Thanks, Eileen."

She left.

He turned to me. "And how may I help you, sir?"

"I wondered if I could ask you a few questions."

"Of course. That's why I'm here." There was just a tad of pomposity in him. People probably laughed behind his back at town meetings. There goes old Walter again with one of his fucking Fourth of July speeches, they'd say. "You'll find our loan rates are the lowest in the state and you'll also find that we have a safety record second to none. The only time this bank was robbed was in 1882 and the robbers were apprehended before they reached the city limits. They are now in state prison."

I think he wanted me to applaud. I wanted to hear him bullmoose his way through a conversation with Stodla. Stodla spoke bluntly and seldom. This man was an automatic chamber of commerce lecturer. Just push him in the belly button and he'd yap for an hour.

"And not only that, but I think you'll find our staff friendlier than any staff anywhere you care to name. We have two telephones, electric lights, and we plan on installing a pump just as soon as the town council gives the go-ahead for the project."

All the time those eyes blinking and driving me crazy.

I said, "Well, that sure is impressive, Mr. Grayson."

"Walter. Please."

"Well, that sure is impressive, Mr. Grayson, but what I

really wanted to know doesn't have anything to do with the bank."

"No?"

"No. It has to do with a man named Stodla and how he ended up staying at your house."

He went from pasty white to scarlet in moments. The eyelids, if anything, fluttered with even more fury. "Exactly who are you?"

"Exactly, I'm Bryce Lamont. You can ask Jed about me. We go way back. I was surprised to see Stodla here. In town, I mean. And alive. I figured somebody would have killed him a long time ago. Every bully gets it eventually."

"Perhaps I should call Chief Pekins."

"I already met him, and we had ourselves a nice little chat, matter of fact. I don't see why he'd want to arrest me after the talk we had, especially for just asking a few harmless questions."

"I have nothing to say. You're wasting your time. And mine."

"I got the impression your wife doesn't exactly consider Stodla to be a member of the family. In fact, she barely spoke to him. Funny you should have a boarder you'd barely speak to."

He stood up. "I have a meeting I need to go to."

"Came up awful sudden, didn't it?"

"You'll be dealing with Jed from now on."

I smiled. "Better him than Stodla. And tell him Stodla's just as thick as he ever was. He started following me around this morning but then I faked him out and started following *him*. It was sort of pathetic. I swear Stodla gets dumber the older he gets."

"Good day, Mr. Lamont."

I guess I wasn't real surprised when he didn't offer to shake my hand again.

Around suppertime, the town folded in on itself. The merchants locked up good and tight, the streets emptied, and the saloons came to noisy life, for those not inclined to domestic tranquility. I'd spent the last hour before closing time at a gunsmith's. I bought a .45. I figured that Jed would come visit me sometime soon and you never knew about Jed. He had a temper that was dangerous because you could see even he didn't know when it was going to erupt. It seemed to have its own mind—and no conscience.

I went up to the kid's room and was about to knock but then I heard a soft voice reading aloud. It was the young doctor.

I decided to go down to the bar, drained two quick beers, and then went and had some supper. It tasted good. This wasn't as bad as Marsha, then. With Marsha, I could barely eat for a year. And when I finally did eat regular again the food didn't taste so good. You want to lose some weight fast, get your heart broken.

It was a pretty night. I went and stood down by the dam. It was chilly. There were some fishermen along the narrow bridge. You could smell their cigar smoke and hear them laughing. I felt like hell again about the kid. He was up there maybe dying and I was all fixated on the girl doctor. The dusk sky was salmon trimmed in gold and you could see the last of the day's lonely birds flying into midnight.

I thought about Jed. It was all so clear and simple when I came here. I wanted my share of the money in any form he cared to pay me with. Then the kid and I would go spend it and have a hell of a time. But things were so complicated now.

There wasn't a whorehouse nearby, but there was a whore and we flopped in her bed in a shack along the river. It took me longer than I wanted to. That's always the way. You're with somebody you like and it ends too fast. You're with somebody you don't care about and you become a champeen-lover, at least endurance-wise.

She took note of the fact that I hadn't kissed her and I said that I was sorry and didn't mean to hurt her feelings, which I didn't, but I never kissed women in these situations. And then she started crying and said, Well if that don't make a gal feel like shit I don't know what does. So I kissed her and held her the way she wanted me to and she said, Thanks mister I really appreciate that. And then I left and walked along the river, full dark now, and watched the moon-gleaming black prairie water and prayed to whatever God there was that my kid brother didn't die.

He was alone and asleep when I got back to his room. I went to my room and fell asleep right away. No word from Jed, which, considering how tired I suddenly was, was good enough for me.

They took the guy out just after midnight.

There was some kind of fuss and it woke me. At first I was afraid it might be the kid. But it was down the hall. I got a lantern lit and went down there.

He was the worst case I'd seen, a middle-aged man who made a funny clacking noise as a nurse and another man helped him down the stairs. At first I couldn't figure out what the clacking was. Then I realized it was his teeth. He smelled bad, too. All the sweating from the times his fever had broken. He was so weak he started to pass out before they got him to the head of the stairs. His eyes were wild, helpless. He looked scared. The man picked him up and carried him.

Another guest was out in the hall. He had his teeth out and was rubbing his peach-fuzz head. "Two of 'em died tonight."

"Where'd you hear that?"

"Saloon."

"That's where I get most of my news, too."

He scowled at me. "You think it's funny?"

"I think it may be bullshit. You know how saloons are. Full of bullshit."

"Well, I already de-bullshitted it."

"How do you go about that?"

"Guy who was telling me said it was four dead. So I cut it in half."

"I see. The scientific method, huh?"

He waved at me with his teeth in his hand. "Go ahead and make jokes. I was in the war. I seen how fast you can die. Thirty, forty men in my regiment." He snapped his fingers. "Like that."

I peeked in at the kid. His breathing was regular. He snored peacefully. I touched my hand to his forehead. Just about the way it should be, maybe even a mite cooler than I would've expected.

I went back to my room. This time sleep didn't come easily. I tried not to think about anything that might help keep me awake. I don't think I got to sleep till near dawn.

SIX

TWO DAYS LATER, on a Friday, Jed Wylie came to the trial.

He looked ten years older than he was, that probably being due to his weight and his gray-streaked hair. Despite, or possibly because of, these changes, he looked more imperious than he ever had. He'd always swaggered about. He had a handsome Roman profile and a sturdy, imposing, manly walk. And he'd always dressed well, though he seemed to have given up his taste for Edwardian fashion. The dark suit he wore was almost funereal. He used a dapper cane with a wolf's head ornament. In the old days, when Jed and Stodla and I were true friends, I used to think Jed's flamboyance was pretty funny. I no longer thought so.

I was seated in the back.

Everything stopped when he came into the courtroom. Everybody watched him. He was not only rich and powerful, his brother had been killed. This only increased the tension. People pointed, whispered. He carried a book under his arm. It was easy to see it was a Bible. Given the cut and color of his suit, he could have been a parson or a mortuary director.

He sat in the second row on the right side of the aisle. He opened his Bible and began to peruse it. There still wasn't much conversation. It was as if your eyes fixed on him of their own volition, whether your brain wanted to or not.

The judge came in ten minutes later. Everybody stood when the judge was announced. When we sat down, the prisoner was escorted into the courtroom. She was a tiny, fetching thing. Even in her gray jail dress, she had a prim eroticism about her—the sort of vulnerability that always got to me even more than a low-cut gown.

It was day four of the trial and more witnesses were being called to the stand to testify this morning. The county attorney became florid, as was his custom, and the defense attorney gently mocked him, to the amusement of the crowd if not the judge or the jury. Both sides had done their homework. This would be a tough call for the jury to decide.

The judge had just called recess for lunch when it happened: I was hungry and getting ready to rush from the courtroom. I didn't figure anything interesting would happen after the judge had closed up shop—but I'd forgotten about Jed's temper.

He'd managed to sit through the morning's proceedings without making a fuss of any kind. He listened without making any kind of noise and without signaling any kind of objection. The county attorney looked his way a few times—as if for approval of a point he'd just made—but other than that, Jed had conducted himself perfectly.

Later, somebody told me that they thought Jenny Rice had

turned around at one point and looked at Jed and that he'd frowned at her. If this happened, I'd somehow missed it.

Whatever led up to it, Jed had had as much as he could handle of the genteel court proceedings. His brother's killer—his brother's *alleged* killer, rather—was not safe in his presence, as he was about to demonstrate.

With no help from his cane, he stepped quickly to the slatted rail dividing the citizens from the judge and jury. He grabbed her by the shoulder, spun her around, and spat fulsomely in her face. Spittle clung to her left eyebrow, dangling there obscenely, and smaller bits stuck to the tip of her nose and the center of her cheek and forehead. And then he slapped her with such force that she was knocked at least two feet backward, into a guard.

"Hey!" shouted a second guard.

But nobody tried to arrest him. There wasn't time.

Jed turned toward the rear of the courtroom and strode swiftly out the exit. If you were in his way, he whacked you with his wolf's-head cane. And I mean whacked you. He got one old bastard right square on his goiter. The aisle was soon cleared for him.

Jenny Rice had collapsed in sobs on the floor. The guards were gently trying to lift her to her feet. Her sobs were ugly. Far worse than hurting her, he'd humiliated her.

I pushed my way outdoors.

The Midwest had its own style. It wasn't western and it wasn't eastern. It was clean and neat and small. For instance, the lone building here meant to impress was a two-story sandstone job that housed law offices and an accounting firm. A man in a jail uniform was sweeping the street in front of the courthouse, and a trolley with a quiet bell was passing by on silver tracks. There were telegraph wires and some poles that connected up the few telephones the town boasted. There were even several moderate electric connectors. The townspeople more resembled Easterners than Westerners, at least in their choice of clothing. No western-style duds, no evidence of guns or knives. Plain clothes for plain people.

It was hard to believe that a few outlaw gangs still operated here, but every once in a while they'd sweep down on a place like this and sometimes hold it hostage for an entire day while they dragged out every valuable they could find. This had happened lately along the section of Iowa that sets on the Mississippi River and borders on Wisconsin; and it had also happened along the Iowa-Missouri border, where the old James and Dalton brothers gangs used to raid. "Last vestiges of the Old West," as one magazine writer had called it.

I'd been meaning to walk right up to Jed and confront him, but he was already in his wagon and pulling away. I wondered what he was waiting for. He knew I was in town, and that he'd be the only reason I'd be here.

I started down the street. In two blocks I passed an alley where two buckboards stood up to the back of a place. Men were loading the wagon. At first I couldn't see what was being loaded, but then the long, slim pine boxes came into clear view. They were preparing to bury people who'd been killed by malaria.

There were six boxes on one wagon, three on the other. A pudgy mortician came out and said, "You boys be sure and take the long way. That's what I'm payin' you for. I don't want these ridin' down Main Street. People are scared enough."

After the wagons left, I went up to him. "How many dead so far?"

"Too many," he said, mopping his face with a sweat-stained white handkerchief.

"That isn't exactly an answer."

"You a newspaperman?"

"Just a citizen."

He shrugged. "I got three of my pine box suppliers workin' around the clock." He took out a cigar and bit off the end and spat it out. "We buried eighteen in the last ten days."

I whistled.

"Yeah, and that ain't all of it. One of 'em was my pop." His eyes glistened suddenly. "You know, I always figured I'd have to do that someday, bury my folks. But you know how it is. You just put off thinkin' about it. Then a year ago my ma died tryin' to save one of her grandkids in the river—he was my brother's kid, five-year-old named Ned . . . he'd wandered out into the water and she was the only one around. She couldn't swim for shit. Nobody in the family could. Strange, isn't it? Not a swimmer in our whole family. Anyway, she got him back to shore but all the excitement gave her a heart attack and she died later that night. And now my pa. Malaria."

A voice called from inside.

"That's my wife. She's got so many forms to fill out for the state—all these malaria deaths and all—she's getting cranky. And she *never* gets cranky. Well, almost never anyway."

I thanked him before he went inside.

I went to a nearby saloon and had one of their free lunches—ham on rye—and two glasses of beer. All anybody talked about was the accelerating number of malaria deaths. There wasn't even any mention of Jed spitting on

Jenny Rice this morning. I guess the prospect of death is more compelling than a criminal proceeding.

I was worried about the kid, of course. This was obviously the killing kind of the disease. Not everybody who contracted it died but a small percentage seemed to.

Maybe just because the subject scared me so much, I started thinking about Jed and Stodla again. Why the hell weren't they approaching me? They should be damned curious about why I was here and how long I planned to stay and what I planned to do.

Then I felt a giant presence next to me.

Up close, Frank Stodla was even bigger than I remembered, like a wall of muscle and mean. He still had his cold, dumb laugh, the one that suggested you were of an inferior species that he in no way took seriously. He was the only man in town who was got up like a cowboy.

He said, "We figured you'da made a move by now."

"I figured *you* would have."

"We don't *have* to make no move, Lamont. Jed's the leading citizen here. He does things in his own good time."

"He didn't look like any leading citizen this morning."

"You mean spitting on that little bitch?"

"Yeah."

"She killed his brother. How do you expect him to act?"

"I thought the jury had to decide if she's guilty."

"Oh, she's guilty, all right. She's one of them clingin' vines. That's why Don couldn't handle her no more. So he gets himself another woman and the Rice gal kills him. Not real hard to figure out."

"Tell Jed I want my share of the money."

His cold, dumb laugh again. "That what this is all about?"

"Yeah, what else would it be about?"

"You come all the way from Denver for that stinkin' little bit of money?"

"Sure looks that way."

"He thought maybe you wanted to shoot him or somethin'. You know, held a grudge like. Hell, he'll pay you the money. No problem."

He whipped out a bowie knife. Splayed his fingers on the bar and said, "Remember this, Lamont?"

I remembered his game: Spread your fingers and let Stodla see how fast he could stab between your fingers. He did this with amazing speed and almost never missed. Almost. He did cut off a man's fingers one night in Kansas City, but nobody's perfect.

"You used to let me do it, remember?"

"Yeah."

A he-man game I used to play with him back in my crazy days. I was a tough guy then, didn't want to show fear. But prison had taught me the sorry truth—I wasn't a tough guy and never would be.

"I'm better than I ever was," he said with his cold smile. People were watching us now.

He did it with his own hand, stabbing between his fingers so fast the knife was nothing more than a blur of motion.

Just to show how good he was, he started stabbing in the opposite direction. Even more people watched.

"You ever cut yourself, mister?" an old man asked.

"Not once. I never make no mistakes."

"He means that in all humility," I said. A few of them got it and laughed.

"If Lamont here is up for it, I'll really show you something. I'll try it on him." He had his audience. Stodla was happy. "So you up for it, Lamont?"

We'd done this routine many, many times back in the days when we'd been friends. He made money on it and we split it.

But there was an intermediary step first.

"How about it, Lamont?"

"You mean you stab the knife between my fingers the way you did yours?" I said this for the benefit of any of the rubes who might not understand what was going on here.

"Just the same's I did my own." He winked at the crowd. "Only faster." They liked his jokes much better than mine.

"C'mon, mister," a couple of them said. "We want to see it."

"You want to do it?" I said to one of them who was urging me on.

He grinned like an embarrassed kid. "Not me. Nossir." And then he looked at his friend, who grinned back.

"Well, since you all seem so interested in seeing me get my fingers chopped off, I guess I don't have much choice."

This time, Stodla winked at the bartender. "You got any glue in case I miss?" There was a thigh-slapper for you. The crowd loved it.

"Put your hand on the bar," Stodla said.

I did so. Reluctantly.

"Now spread your fingers."

I did so. Reluctantly.

"Now say yer prayers." Another thigh-slapper. I think at that moment the crowd would have elected Stodla president of the United States. He'd found his flock and he was about to fleece them.

"Ready, Lamont?"

"Ready."

Of course, just because we didn't like each other anymore, and just because there wasn't any money riding on this particular part of the con, he might just get mercenary and slice one of my fingers off. He was certainly capable of it. The way he used to beat up whores, he was capable of anything.

"You boys say a prayer fer Lamont here."

They all grinned obediently.

"Here goes."

I closed my eyes. I always used to do that in the old days for effect, so I figured I might as well do it now.

He did, in fact, work faster on my fingers than he had his own. He went left-right first then right-left. He didn't so much as touch my fingers with his blade.

"I'll be a sonofabitch," the bartender said, picking his nose. "You sure are good at that, mister."

"And you're good at diggin' out those boogers."

More laughter. The bartender wiped his picking finger off on his apron. He flushed.

"Well, I guess that's about it," Stodla said. He was anticipating the reaction he'd get. He'd brought them to the carnival midway and only ended up showing them one attraction. They all sighed to show their disappointment. This was fun.

One of them said, "I'll let you try it on me." Hell, he really had them. They were willing to sacrifice their own fingers just so the heady fun would continue.

In all, six of them stepped forward. It took about twenty minutes. One guy stepped up and put his hand on the bar and then backed out. Another guy made grotesque faces all the time Stodla was working the knife. Everybody laughed, including me. Those faces he made were something to see.

And then it was over again. Or so they thought.

Stodla said, "Well, gentlemen, it's been fun. But I'm afraid the old bear's run out of tricks."

"You don't know no other tricks with that knife of yours?" a young rube asked.

"'Fraid not, friends." He even used the same dialogue he'd used years before. And he turned back to me and his beer. He took a couple of swallows and looked at me and said, "You don't suppose this is the kinda crowd that'd go for a blindfold trick?"

"I don't think so," I said. "I don't think they've got the stomach for the blood."

They knew they were being had—all chuckles and mile-wide grins—and they loved it. The carnival had come back to town.

"What trick you thinkin' of, mister?" a geezer asked.

"Well, for one thing, the last time I tried it, I ended up in jail," Stodla said.

"Jail? What the hell they'd put you in jail for?" a red-headed fellow said.

Stodla held up his two middle fingers. "I was usin' the blindfold, see, and—"

"You do that knife business *blindfolded*?" a large blond-bearded man asked in a pleasingly astonished voice.

"I try," Stodla said humbly. "It don't always work."

"Blindfolded," the bartender said, shaking his head slowly. "I'll be damned. Now *that* I'd like to see."

"Anyway," Stodla said, still holding his middle two fingers, "I probably had a little too much swampwater in me to try the trick at this particular time. But the guy kept wantin' to bet me I couldn't do it and we found somebody who'd slap his hand down on the bar and—well, I missed. Took off both his fingers right about here." He indicated a point equidistant between knuckles and joints.

"Have to be a crazy sonofabitch to put his hand down there for that one," the redheaded fellow said with a grin.

Stodla said, "Aw, it don't come cheap."

"You mean you *charge* to see it?" a balding man said.

"I don't charge exactly. But I do make everybody in the bar give the man with the hand a gold dollar. That's only fair. He's takin' all the risk and if I cut him there's gonna be medical costs. How many men's in here?" Stodla did a quick count. "Twenty-six. You three over at the table there. You three be willing to pay up a dollar each?"

"We get to pick the blindfold?" one of the men at the table half-shouted.

"Sure do. Don't make no nevermind to me."

The man consulted his friends at the table and then said, "Yeah, we'll put up the money."

They grabbed their beers and stood up and came over.

"If any of you men here would like to help me, show me your hand. Otherwise I'll ask Mr. Lamont to help me out with this one."

"What happens if you cut him?"

And that's when I added the final dramatic stroke. I took the .45 from inside my suit jacket and put the end of the barrel right against Stodla's head. "He so much as nicks me with that blade of his, I'll kill him right on the spot."

"Here, now," the bartender said. "You can't carry no gun in this town without getting permission from the chief of police personally."

"Shut up, Al," the large bearded man said to him.

"We want to see this," another man said.

"You'd really shoot him?" the redheaded fellow asked me.

"Just wait and see," I said.

"Well," Stodla said, "I'll let you boys pick out the blind-

fold and put it on me in case some of you might think it's
fake or somethin'."

"There's got to be some kinda catch to this," a man said.

"Nope," Stodla said. "I'm blindfolded and I'm looking
away."

"You're lookin' away?"

"Yep. So even if I *could* see through the blindfold—
which I can't—I couldn't see what I was doin' anyway."

"I'll be jiggered."

"I'll be *double*-jiggered."

They got him a heavy bar rag and they folded it three
times over. Stodla bent down so they could tie it around
his head. Then they adjusted the blindfold quickly, shaping
the cloth so that they were sure it covered his eyes completely. He couldn't see over or under it. It was already
clear he couldn't see through it.

"Now show us how you're gonna turn your head."

"You'll have to get everything in place," Stodla said.
"You ready, Lamont?"

"I'm ready." I took my place at the bar and splayed my
hand out.

Men kept walking up to him, giving him the finger, pretending to jab him in the eye, waving at him and grinning
like silly boys. All to make sure he couldn't see.

They put him in place at the bar. He picked up his knife.
He reached out, groping his way to my fingers. Then he
turned his head completely away.

"Gosh."

"That poor sumbitch with his fingers."

The bearded man laughed. "You mean that poor sumbitch
without his fingers."

Then everybody laughed.

The balding man checked the blindfold again. "You sure you want to do this?"

"I'm willin' if Lamont is," Stodla said.

"Let's just get it over with," I said.

"I got to go over his hands a few times," Stodla said.

This wasn't part of a routine. This was serious. He really *did* have to go over my fingers. Make sure where they were in relation to him, and how far apart they were. He had great instincts for this. Or he used to anyway. I hoped he still did.

He went over my fingers six, seven times.

"Maybe he's fallin' in love with that guy, way he keeps touchin' his hand," the redheaded guy said.

Laughter.

"They start *holdin'* hands, I'm gonna get damn suspicious," said a short, grizzled old man.

More laughter.

"You gentlemen ready?" Stodla said.

"Ready!" They shouted as one.

He passed his fingers over mine one more time. His head was so big the knot in the blindfold looked as if it was going to pop at any moment.

He took a deep breath. Changed his knife from left hand to right. Took another deep breath. "You understand, boys, this ain't gonna be anywhere near as fast as when I can see."

They all grumbled agreement. They were getting impatient. They just wanted to see him cut the shit out of my fingers.

He raised the knife. The bartender made a little sign of the cross. I guess not everybody wanted to see me get cut.

He brought the knife down. Between my thumb and forefinger. Usually he struck right in the center between my digits. This one had come very close to slicing the inside of my thumb.

I just watched my fingers. He did the rest pretty fast, considering the circumstances. And then—pleased with himself—he reversed course and ran through my fingers backwards.

"I'll be dogged," one old guy muttered.

"I'll be double-dogged," the large, bearded man added.

"That scared the shit out of me," the bartender said when Stodla was finished.

"Not a scratch," a young fellow said. "Right, mister, not a scratch on you?"

I said, "That's right. Not a scratch." I held up my hand for inspection.

Stodla took the blindfold off. Men were clapping him on the back. He was enjoying himself, grinning and knocking back the various drinks the bartender was setting before him, all bought and paid for by various customers.

An hour later, we left the saloon.

He said, "You got a lot steadier nerves than you used to have, Lamont."

"I'm older. And dumber."

"Tell you the truth, I hadn't done that in a long time. Years. Wasn't sure if I could still pull it off." He reached in the pocket of his trousers and brought out a fistful of gold dollars. "Here's your cut."

"Thanks." I stuffed the dollars in my pocket.

Many nights, the money we'd made performing the blindfold trick was all we had for supper and lodging. On good nights, we'd have a nice hotel room each. On bad nights, we'd sleep on benches by a river somewhere.

We came to the end of Main Street and stopped.

"You'll tell him what I want?"

"Damn right I will, Lamont. Ain't right, you not getting your money for that job. Especially since you're the one who did the time."

"You really think he'll see it my way?"

Stodla shrugged. "Sure I do. He's the bank president now. He's got all kinds of pressure on him from all kinds of people. He'll want to make it right. You're one problem he don't need right now."

I put out my hand. He was still the big, naïve sheepdog. I wasn't sure he was as crazy as he had been in the old days. "I wish I had your faith in people, Stodla. All the shit you've been through in your life, I don't see how you can still trust anybody."

"Well, I trust people because if they hurt me bad enough, I'll kill 'em. They know that and I know that and maybe that's why they don't try'n take advantage of me the way they do people like—" He left it unfinished.

"People like me, you were going to say?"

"People ain't scared enough of you, Lamont. They don't trust you. But they ain't scared of you. And that makes a difference. It really does."

We shook hands. Maybe he was right. Maybe I needed to be scarier.

"Well, I got to go see my brother," I said. "I'll wait to hear from you."

"Probably sometime tonight," he said.

"Thanks, Stodla," I said.

I'd walked maybe half a block back toward the center of town when the gunfire started. Several loud shots fired in quick succession. And then I saw a man in the bank door, backing out with a gun in hand. He had a red kerchief over his face. Just then he squeezed off two more shots.

SEVEN

FOUR HORSES CAME out of the alley. Three of the horses had empty saddles. The rider leading them wore a kerchief over his face and fired a Winchester into the street to keep the curious away.

Two robbers came out of the bank. The first man, who'd backed out, was already running to his horse. The second one was firing back into the bank. The way he was shooting, you could tell he wasn't aiming at anything in particular. He just wanted to keep busybodies away, too.

Stodla started after them. But I grabbed his sleeve. "You crazy?"

He pulled away. "Jed's my friend. That's his bank they're robbin'."

"He's got a Winchester, in case you hadn't noticed."

"Fuck 'em. I'm goin' after him anyway."

He lunged forward in the dusty street. I got ahead of him and tripped him. A ballerina he wasn't. He fell down with all the grace of a lassoed mule.

All three of the bank robbers were shooting now. It was a good way to keep the streets cleared. Windows shattered, animals cried, people screamed; old men tried to run fast, young men tried to look tough even while they were hiding. In Texas, you still heard sounds like this, but Wisconsin?

This was about the time the chief came lurching out of his station. He had a Winchester and he wasn't inclined to dawdle. He was a much better shot that I'd expected and wasn't afraid of them, either. He positioned himself right on the boardwalk, a perfect target.

He got one of the robbers clean in the shoulder. The rider wavered a moment, looking confused, as if he couldn't quite make up his mind if the shot was real or imaginary. Then, without any warning, he pitched forward. I figured he was headed for the ground. But one of his partners grabbed him by the hair and pulled him back up. Then the same man took the reins of the wounded man's horse, sprayed a few more shots around the empty street, and started north out of town.

The third rider, who also had a Winchester, held Pekins at bay by charging him. He was a brave bastard, I had to give him that. He came flying at Pekins, his mount spooked and half-crazed with all the gun noise, and put two bullets right in the chief's shooting arm. The rifle flew from Pekins's hand. The force of the shots knocked him back against the front of the police station. But the rider kept coming until he got close enough to raise his foot and kick Pekins square and hard right on the jaw. Pekins was gone in an instant. That kind of kick had to hurt as much as the bullets had, maybe even more.

Then the rider did some more general shooting and rode out after his northbound partners.

A silence began to fill the street. It sounded pretty damned beautiful after all the clamor. People even began to file back into the street. I helped Stodla up on his feet.

"You sonofabitch, you shouldn't ought to've done that, Lamont."

But I didn't have time to answer because the silence was suddenly no more. Shots behind the bank, then shouts; more shouts. A bank clerk ran out on the boardwalk and shouted, "There's a wounded one and he just got away!"

"This time you ain't stoppin' me, Lamont," Stodla growled, "and God help ya if ya try."

I didn't try to stop him this time, but I ran after him.

Stodla went for the alley, which is where the robber had probably fled. Three men with rifles worked the narrow, dusty alley. A golden tomcat looked at us with great disdain.

"Everybody divide up!" one of the men ordered. "Start checkin' out the backs of these places. He's probably hidin' in one of them."

Made sense. If he was wounded and couldn't travel fast, the robber probably had to find some sort of hiding place where he could hopefully get some strength and energy back, and maybe sneak out when night fell.

The alley ran behind Main Street. We knocked on all the back doors of the various retail places. None of the people who answered had seen or heard anybody run in. Most of the merchants had their guns drawn. This dime novel bunk you read about helpless merchants—well, you rile up a bunch of merchants and you'll find out just how helpless they really are. Just about every merchant I've ever known keeps several guns handy. And that goes for Wisconsin as well as Wyoming or Idaho.

Stodla was getting angrier by the minute. He kept cursing, sneering. "He give me a life here, Lamont. That's what you don't understand. When he settled down—gave up the kinda life we was leadin'—he told me to settle down, too. I even got my own little cabin along the lake."

"Then why do you live with the Graysons?"

He grunted. "I'll explain it to you sometime."

Then, looking afraid that I might pursue the subject, he moved away from me again and headed into the back door of the blacksmith's.

Now he really had me curious.

The next three places I searched were a saddlery, a dentist's office, and a real estate office. The back door of the real estate office was unlocked. Nobody was working inside. Just made for a robber on the run. I thought I heard a noise in a closet and spent three minutes shouting at the closet door. Finally, I got brave as hell and kicked the door so it popped open. There was nothing inside, which was when the real estate man came in and gave me hell for damaging his door. I said, "There's a robber loose."

"I couldn't give a damn, friend. Now you get the hell out of here."

Later on, some would say the scream came before the shot while others would insist that the shot came before the scream. Personally, I couldn't tell you and it doesn't much matter anyway.

I recognized the scream. I don't know how, but I did. And I took off running to the end of the block where the hotel was, where my kid brother was staying.

More gunfire. Six, seven shots. Then a man ran out on the small landing of the hotel back stairs and said, "Newsome got him! He killed the robber! Got him right through the eye! You should see it!"

I headed into the hotel, still thinking about the scream I'd heard. I was sure it had been Laura Westcott's scream.

But what was I worried about? If the robber was dead, it was all over.

I went up to the third floor of the hotel and was out of breath by the time I got to Paul's door.

There was a man laid out on the floor in the doorway. As advertised, he had a bullet in his eye. The socket was filled with blood and pieces of eyeball. He had a gun in his hand. At this point it wasn't doing him a lot of good.

The doctor was in there with the kid. She had a couple of extra pillows under his head. He looked wild bad, his eyes going everywhere, his entire body jumping and jerking like a cocaine addict on the downside. He kept saying crazy things that made no sense, talking to our mother.

She looked back at me just once. She was as scared as he was. Paul had bullet wounds in his chest. There was a lot of blood.

He stopped twitching then. He lay absolutely still and stared at the ceiling. He started talking to our mother again—he told her he was gonna go to town with Pa and they'd bring her something sweet back—and then he started talking about an old Border collie we'd had by the name of Jim. Then he started jumping and jerking again.

Without turning around, the doc gestured to me. I stepped over the dead man, making sure to kick him hard as I did so, and then went to stand next to the kid.

I didn't want to. I knew he wouldn't even recognize I was there and I was right. I said his name a few times softly but he didn't even blink his eyes. He just kept staring at the ceiling and talking to people who had preceded him into death, like Scottie, who lived the next farm over and had been his best friend, and Dora Ann, who he'd been sweet on from church on Sundays.

I was glad he was delirious. It'd gentle his passing for

him. Crossing over with Mom and Pop, and old Jim and
Scottie and Dora Ann, there couldn't be a better way to go.
Just at the end there, I knelt down next to him and took his
hand. Still no recognition. But I didn't care.

"I'll miss you, kid," I said in a low voice. "I'll think
about you all the time. I never should've brought you along
with me. I told you that, and I was right."

And then he let go. His hand opened, and mine slid away.
And then his whole body went slack.

I couldn't rightly tell you what happened in the next five
minutes. Somehow I ended up on the back porch, smoking
a tailor-made cigarette and taking pulls from a pint bottle
of bourbon somebody'd been kind enough to put in my
hand.

Then she was next to me, the doctor, and she was taking a pull from the same bottle, and we just stood there for
a time, hardly aware of all the activity below and around
us: the undertaker bringing a wagon and two stretchers, the
deputies interviewing hotel guests and workers, the hotel
clerk and a maid lugging mops and buckets up the stairs.

We didn't say anything, the doctor and I. She cried a little. But I was too wrapped up in my own grief to comfort
her.

The undertaker's men took the robber's body down first.
I wanted to kick him in the head again, kick him so hard
that his head came apart in three or four bloody sections.

When she saw him, the doc said, "They were chasing
him through the hotel. Our door was open. He came in and
said he'd kill us if we said a word. Paul got the shakes real
bad. He reached across to get his medicine and knocked the
nightstand over. That's how the deputies figured out the man
was in our room. The first thing he did was shoot Paul

twice in the chest. He would've shot me but the deputies opened up with a rifle and killed him through the door.

"The funny thing was that your brother was getting a lot better," Laura said, handing the bottle to me. "The malaria, I mean."

"Really?"

She nodded. "He would've been sick a long time. But he was past the danger of dying."

The deputy came over and talked to her. She told him what had happened. He said he was sorry a couple of times. Pekins had done a good job training his boys.

When they were finished, she turned back to me. "I need to get back to the clinic. What're you going to do?" She looked as weary and sad as she probably felt.

"Get drunk."

"You think that'll help?"

I shrugged. "It may not help but I don't know what else to do."

She smiled bitterly. "Yeah, You're probably right." Then she looked directly at me and said, "I'm going to say something very unprofessional to you."

"Oh?"

"I was very much in love with Paul."

Her words startled me. "He was just a kid." I still couldn't get used to the idea that my kid brother had been thinking of getting married.

"So am I, Mr. Lamont. He was six months older than me." She looked off at some distant point. "I've been out here two years and I think I've been squired around by every eligible man between the ages of twenty and sixty in the entire county. And I didn't have the slightest interest in any of them. But Paul—" Her eyes glistened. "It was kind of funny. I always thought it would be like a Sir Walter

Scott book. The big bold knight riding up and saving me. But it wasn't like that at all. From the moment we met a few weeks ago, we got along almost like a brother and sister. He told me things he said he'd never told anybody and I told him things about myself *I'd* certainly never shared with anyone. And we laughed and I read stories to him. And about the fifth day I'd known him, he said, 'I think I'm in love with you, Laura.' And I started to laugh and say he was just being silly, but then I realized I felt the same way, too. I really was in love with him."

She crossed her arms as if she had just gotten a chill. "Up in his room when he got sick, we would joke about me keeping him sick so I wouldn't ever have to let him go. And he said I didn't have to worry about that because he was planning on staying right here in town. With me. I had two men before him, a husband and a lover, and they both beat me up and treated me like a slave. I'd given up on men till I met Paul." Her eyes returned to me. "What I really want to do is go home and cry. But I can't because then everybody in town'd say women doctors aren't as tough as men and I have a lot of pride in what I do, Mr. Lamont. So I'll go to the clinic and do my job and be tough. But when I get home tonight, I'm going to be a helpless mess. I'll tell you that."

I wondered what it would be like to be loved by a woman like this. A clean, good, sound, tenacious, wise sort of love, the kind that keeps people together their whole lives.

I said, "I could bring a bottle by."

She shook her head. "I need to be alone, Mr. Lamont."

"I wish you'd call me Bryce."

"Bryce, then." She sighed. "Now it's back to the clinic. They brought in four more malaria cases last night. It's starting to get scary."

"More deaths?"

"Two more. And by the end of the day, I'm sure there'll be two more than that."

Then she did something I half-wished she hadn't. She took my hand and touched it to her cheek and said, "We both loved him, Bryce. And that gives us something very important in common."

Then she was gone.

EIGHT

THE FIRST PERSON I looked up was Krohn. If there were any rumors in town about the identity of the bank robbers, he'd have them.

I found him on a bench at the depot. There was a short-haul train there taking people to Milwaukee. He said, "Heard about your brother."

"Yeah."

"You gonna leave it up to the law?"

"You like watching people suffer, don't you, Krohn?"

He smiled at me with brown stubs of teeth. "Can't honestly say I mind it. 'Bout the only thing a feller can do is watch other people and their troubles."

He had a pint of something and took a swig. "I'd offer you some but I'm low on money."

"That was one of the things I wanted to talk to you about."

"Money?"

"Yeah."

The brown simile again. "Well, I'll make it easy for you. I ain't got any and I ain't likely *to* get any."

"You hear anything about the robbery?"

"Heard there *was* one. Heard there were four of them. Heard they cleaned out the bank. Heard one of them got wounded and rode off with the rest. And heard one got killed."

"And that's all you've heard?"

"So far."

They were like paintings, the faces in the short-haul passenger windows. The ladies wore big picture hats and the men looked miserable in their celluloid collars and suits. They were farm people mostly. You could tell that by their sunburned faces. They'd stay at a Milwaukee hotel with no whores but plenty of cockroaches, and they'd eat in a restaurant where the city inspector got bribed the first day of every month, and they'd take in an entertainment or two that boasted Broadway talent too old for anything but the road. They'd have their pictures taken and buy some silly gifts and they'd walk up and down the river downtown where the view was about as spectacular as a view gets in this part of the country; and then, this being four or five days into their trip, they'd start missing their kids and their farm and their own beds, and they'd be eager to see another red short-haul all ready to hie them back home.

It was the kind of life I'd spent all my years mocking but now I wondered. Paul and Laura Westcott would've fit nicely into that sort of life.

Krohn said, "You kin always hire somebody."

"For what?"

"To track 'em down and kill 'em. If you don't want to do it yourself."

"If I wanted them dead that bad, I'd do it myself."

He laughed. "You restore my faith in humanity, Lamont. Here I was startin' to figure you for some kinda pussy. Men kill your brother and you just let them ride out."

I took my wallet from my suit jacket and counted out a considerable amount. Considerable to him, anyway. "I want you to listen. And listen good. There's somebody in town who knows these men. Job like this, there's always somebody local who helps out. Takes a little piece of the pie for his trouble. That's who I want you to find."

"You gonna kill him?"

"Maybe."

He shook his head. "You know the last time we had a good killin' in this town?"

"When?"

"Six years ago. And it was two drunk Injuns with knives cuttin' the livin' shit out of each other. But that don't hardly count, them bein' Injuns and all. I can't remember when a white man killed another white man."

"That's a sad tale, Krohn."

"Yer makin' fun of me, but it *is* a sad tale. What kinda town don't have killin's?"

"The kind of town most folks want to live in."

"Not folks *I* know." Then he sat back and looked at the short-haul windows. "I'm try'n to figure out which'd be the best ones to screw."

Of six windows, four were filled with women.

"Which ones you figure?" I said.

"I'd say number two, even though you can't really see her tits, the winda kinda cuts them off. And winda number five. Lookit them lips. Them's *lips*, boy. You don't hardly *never* see lips like that, let me tell you you don't."

"They're nice, all right. But I like window one."

"Hell, you can see her tits and she ain't got any. And her nose is too big."

"Look at her neck."

"Her neck? Now who gives a shit about her neck?"

"It's graceful. Like her fingers. I saw her touch her hat a while ago. She has long, graceful fingers."

"Fingers? *Fingers*? Who gives a shit about her fingers?"

"I'll bet she's got good ankles and speaks softly and is very sweet when you're done making love. She also has beautiful gray eyes."

Krohn laughed. "Man, you are somethin' else, you know that? You may be a pussy after all."

I laughed, too. I kept trying not to think about the kid, and this pointless bullshit palaver was doing the trick. At least for now. It was fun to get old Krohn all revved up— I imagined he enjoyed using me as a foil just as much as I enjoyed using him—you do all sorts of things to forestall grief because you know that when it grabs you, it ain't ever going to let you go.

"You know that doctor?" he asked.

"Westcott?" I said.

"Yeah."

"I think they was sweet on each other."

"Yeah?"

"I seen them in the park one night. On a bench. He had his arm around her and she had her head on his shoulder."

"She's very pretty."

"I should've figured *you'd* like her. No tits."

I laughed. The hell of it was he really meant all this about breasts. It was sad but it was fun in an outrageous sort of way. You could imagine him in an art museum filled with classical paintings, judging each one by how big the tits were on this painting or that. The East Coast boys would love him.

I wired six people about Paul dying and then I went over and picked out a coffin and arranged for a minister, who seemed unhappy that Paul had been a heathen.

"Look, you can bury him or not. I can always find somebody else."

"Yes, I'm sure you'd prefer a Druid if you could find one."

At least he had a sense of humor; he also had a sense of commerce. He'd bury him without a formal sermon for ten dollars, fifteen with a sermon.

"The sermons I've heard, it should be the other way around."

"I beg your pardon?"

"The charge should be fifteen without a sermon and ten with one."

He finally caught it and laughed. "I'm sensing that you're not a deeply spiritual person."

"I'm sensing the same thing about you, Reverend."

He frowned. Then, "Tell me a few things about him so I can mention them."

"I told you. I don't want a sermon."

"This isn't a sermon. This is just a moment at the casket. Free of charge."

I shook my head. "Forget it. I hate it when ministers pretend they've known somebody when they haven't. He was a smart, decent young man. Anything else is private."

"A smart, decent young man. Then that's what I'll say."

"Free of charge," I said. "I'm impressed."

Around four that afternoon, I was sitting in the rocking chair in my hotel room, pulling on a pint of rye, when I got the chills. The first thing I put it down to was Paul dying. It's funny the things your body can do to you. You may not be consciously mourning but your body is. That's what I figured was going on. I had a dog die on me one time and I came down with the worst head cold I'd ever had. Two weeks the sonofabitch went on.

I went to bed and drifted off to sleep. I dreamed of Paul. We were kids again and our folks were still alive and it was some kind of holiday because Mom had made this special cake and some of our same-age cousins were there and we were having sack races and I was feeling again the crush I got every summer on my cousin Audra.

The knock was hard and abrupt. The caller didn't wait for an answer. He just came right in. I hazily reached for my gun on the nightstand but he was quick. He grabbed my wrist, wouldn't let me pick the gun up.

"No call for that, Lamont." Voice from the past. Rich, deep, masculine. But naturally so. No affectation. "You never could shoot worth a shit anyway."

I started to wake up then.

He produced a silver flask from his back pocket and tossed it on the bed. I put a sizable dent in the contents.

"Paul had malaria when he was shot. I was around him a lot. You may not want to drink out of that flask after me."

He smiled. "Considerate bastard, aren't you? Well, for your peace of mind—and mine—I'd say that alcohol would kill off any germs."

"I forgot, Jed. You know everything."

"Not everything," he said. "Just the things that are worth knowing."

He hooked his thumbs into the pockets of his vest and smirked at me. He was a master at smirking. He knew a joke not even God knew. And he didn't plan on sharing it.

The weight he'd gained, the graying hair, the ever more expansive way he carried himself, you could see him as a banker or a politician. He'd kiss a baby and pat the mother on the bottom while he was doing it.

"Good old Dartmouth," I said.

Jed Wylie, as the elder son of the richest man in the valley, had spent two years back east. The folks at Dartmouth had seen fit to expel him when they caught him running a prostitution ring out of his dormitory. He didn't need the money. He just wanted something to do. And nothing excited Jed as much as something illicit or illegal. I recognized like kind. I was sort of the same way myself.

He pulled a chair up and sat down and took a drink from the flask. He slammed his hand to his head and said, "Aw, shit, Lamont. It's got me! The fever! I'm dyin'!"

That was another thing. He loved to clown. Even if nobody else thought he was especially funny, he did.

Then, "I'm sorry to hear about your brother."

"So am I."

"He was just a kid only time I met him in Missouri."

"He was a kid when he died today. A good kid."

"He had a nice-lookin' gal. That doctor." He paused. "So what comes next?"

"Find them," I said.

"And then?"

I shrugged. "Kill a couple of them. Maybe all of them."

"The one who shot your brother's already dead."

"I figure Paul was worth at least two or three of them."

"You sound serious."

"I am."

He took another sip from the flask. "They cleaned me out. Damned near everything." He looked at me. "Fortunately, I took this out this morning after I saw you in court."

He pitched a heavy white envelope on my lap. "What's this?" I asked.

"The money I owe you."

It was all there. One-third of fifty thousand dollars. Big green bills. "I can't believe you had a guilty conscience."

"Too much on my mind now that I've got to take over the bank. I don't want somebody from my past roaming around the streets holding a grudge against me. Easier to just pay you off and send you on your way."

I thumbed through the money the other way. "I saw you spit on that woman in court this morning."

"I should've shot her. That little bitch. I just hope the jury can see through her."

"Then there's no question she shot him?"

"Not in my mind. And not in the minds of anybody who can think clearly, either. Who else would've killed him?"

"They said he had enemies."

Jed laughed. "All bankers have enemies. Especially when you have an economy as turbulent as ours has been the last five, six years. But that doesn't mean bankers get shot."

"Some bankers get shot."

"Not my brother. Not by any customer anyway. She shot him plain and simply because he was leaving her. He'd finally been able to see how narrow and selfish and petty Jenny is."

He shrugged and continued, "He was a good boy. He took everything from my mother—looks, breeding, instincts. He made it all the way *through* Dartmouth. And when he had customers who couldn't pay, he'd lend them their payments out of his own pocket sometimes. He even paid for a little girl's operation one time."

I swung my legs off the bed. "No enemies?"

"No enemies. That's one reason I'm sure it was Jenny Rice who killed him."

"What's another reason?"

"She was the only person in the valley who could get away with it and she knew it."

"And how would that be?"

"Everybody loves her. They can't see behind the mask. They think she's a fucking saint. But they're finally starting to pick her apart in court. I figure a few more days and the jury will vote to put her in prison the rest of her life."

This time, I swigged from my own supply of booze. "I figured you'd want to see her hang."

He shook his head and frowned. "This is Wisconsin, my friend, not Texas. We don't hang ladies here, especially not ones of such delicate dispositions. I'd do the job personally but they wouldn't let me."

I kept thinking how disappointing all this was. Sometimes in prison I didn't have much else to think about other than how I was going to get even with Jed. It was going to be dramatic and it was probably going to be bloody and it would give me enough satisfaction to last me the rest of my life.

I sure didn't expect him to wake me up and give me a drink and toss an envelope full of money at me.

I sure didn't plan on sitting on the edge of a bed, smoking a cigarette, and commiserating with him over the deaths of our respective brothers.

I wondered if he'd maybe changed. But then I thought no. People evolved but they didn't really change, not deep down. I hadn't. And I doubted Jed had either.

He said, "Maybe you could pick up on that doctor."

It was as if he'd been peering into my thoughts. A gentleman would never have suggested that I try to take the place of my brother with his woman. That didn't seem to bother Jed at all. He saw nothing wrong with it.

"She was my brother's girl."

"Pussy is pussy."

I reached over and picked up my .45 and aimed it right at his face.

"Oh, shit, Lamont, don't tell me you've gone soft on me." Jed looked disappointed in me.

"She was my brother's girl," I repeated slowly.

"Okay, she was your brother's girl."

"I want an apology."

"Are you fucking crazy?"

"The mood I'm in, Jed, I just might blow your fucking face off."

He shook his head. "I give you a drink, I pay you back the money I owed you, I tell you I'm sorry about your brother. And you get all spooky over some joke I make?"

"I want an apology,"

He waved a beefy arm. "Then I apologize. All right? I fucking apologize! Prison sure didn't do your head any good, Lamont, I'll sure tell you that much."

"By rights, you should've been in there with me."

He laughed. "Boy, have you pumped *your*self full of shit."

"Meaning what?"

"Meaning if you'd crawled out the window first, the way Stodla and I did, would you have waited around for me?"

All the time in prison I'd felt sorry for myself, deserted. No honor among thieves. They'd left me there. But now, listening to the way he put it, I knew he was right.

"Would you've come back after me?" he said.

"I guess not."

"You 'guess,' my ass. Hell, no, you wouldn't have. And I wouldn't have *expected* you to."

I put the gun down.

"You wouldn't have shot me anyway. You're not a killer and neither am I. We're artists of the long con."

"Is Stodla a killer?" I asked, curious about his response.

"He's too sentimental to be a killer. Give him a sad story and he'll back down. I've seen it happen and so have you. Remember that guy in Montana, you and I were working a con on him for his land, and he told Stodla how his little girl had had some kind of cancer of the leg and Stodla wouldn't let us go through with it then? Hell, you didn't want to go through with it, either, come to think about it."

"Did you?"

He shrugged. "Everybody's got some kind of hard luck story, Lamont. God didn't mean for any of us to be happy."

"You don't think I can kill those holdup men?"

"I doubt it."

"You said you wanted to kill Jenny Rice."

He laughed again. "We're shootin' the shit, Lamont. Two middle-aged fuckups tryin' to impress each other. I'd like to slap her around for twenty, thirty minutes but to actually kill her—I don't think I could actually do it. And I don't think you could actually kill those holdup men. It just isn't what we do, Lamont. We want the thrill of separating people from their money, not their lives. That's a different breed of cat altogether."

And maybe he was right. In prison I'd known a couple of killers. And as ordinary as they were in most ways, there was some difference you could sense about them, some shadow that passed across their eyes from time to time. One of them, he'd killed a couple of kids, and some of the other cons castrated him and then set him on fire down there. The other killer was a gunny. Everybody was afraid of him. He liked to say he'd killed people with every kind of weapon you could think of and he could kill you with his bare hands if he needed to. And we believed him. Even the toughest of us walked wide of him. We were all sort of relieved the day they finally hanged him.

He stood up. "Need to get back to the bank."

"What's a banker do when he hasn't got any money?"

He grinned. "Goes and finds some." Then, "You want to shake hands?"

"I guess not." I still didn't trust him.

"I told Stodla you wouldn't. Told him you'd still hold it against us."

"Not us. You."

"Why just me?"

"Because you're smart and he isn't."

"I guess that makes sense. At least sort of." The grin. "I'll tell Stodla you think he's a moron."

I couldn't help it. I laughed.

"Stop by the bank before you leave town. I'll buy you a meal."

"Who said I was leaving town?"

He stared at me for a moment. Then, "I know better than to say you might be stayin' because of that lady doctor. So what else'd keep you around?"

"The holdup men."

"Yeah, well, they're well on their way west by now. You can bet on that."

"I guess we'll see, won't we?"

He smiled. "Yeah, Lamont, I guess we will." Then, "You don't look so good. You feelin' all right?"

"Just fine," I said. "Just fine."

NINE

WE BURIED THE kid the next day. The preacher threw the dirt on the coffin and Laura Westcott started crying. I went to put my arm around her but she eased away from me.

The preacher took due note of this. A smile parted his lips momentarily. He was happy to see me spurned, given the way I'd talked to him yesterday.

It was a clear, fine day. They filled in the grave, making small talk and jokes as they did so. That irritated me at first—you want the whole world to stop when it's one of your own—but then I realized the kid had been nothing to them.

I went up on the hill and smoked a cigarette. Laura stayed down by the grave. At one point I could see her talking to him, in that sort of self-conscious way people talk to dead people. I wondered what she was saying to him. And then she started crying again. When I went down there this time, I didn't try to put my arm around her.

"He's really dead," she said. She was talking more to herself than me. You could see nightcrawlers in the shovel-turned earth. I shuddered when I saw them; actually shuddered. It was for the kid and myself as well.

She looked up at me. "I shouldn't have pulled away from you like that. "

"That's all right."

"It's just I—I don't know you. And I'm shy about people touching me."

"It's fine. Really."

She looked at the turned earth again. "You'd think that all the dying I've seen lately . . . I would've handled this better."

"You loved him,"

Her head rose again and those soft beautiful eyes rested on my face. "Yes, I did. I loved him very much." I thought she was going to cry again. "We were talking about having a baby. Did he tell you that?"

"No. But I knew he was hoping you'd get married soon."

"We even had a plot of land picked out where we were going to build our home." She described where it was. "There's just a shack there now, but the house would have been our place. We were going to have three kids."

I smiled. "He was just a kid himself."

She shook her head. "Not really. He had that baby face but inside he was very grown up. He let himself be kind and he let himself be sensitive and he wasn't ashamed of that."

I said something I'd been thinking about through the night. "I was the one who sent him here. If it hadn't been for me, he'd still be alive."

"But if you hadn't sent him here, I wouldn't ever have met him, Mr. Lamont."

"Please, call me Bryce."

"Bryce. I wouldn't have met him otherwise. And now I'll have him the rest of my life. And I'll see him again. I'm a believer, Bryce, not necessarily a Christian. I believe in all religions that teach kindness and charity and mercy. And I can't believe God put us here for just this—all the suffering I see every day."

"Jed Wylie tells me God doesn't mean for us to be happy."

"Jed Wylie," she said, and shook her head. "Did he also tell you that he's been chasing my skirts ever since I came to town?"

I smiled. "That's Jed."

She didn't smile. "I realize I'm not unattractive. But I also realize that a man should be faithful to his wife. I feel sorry for her every time I see her, as if I've betrayed her in some way. She's a very sweet woman. She works a lot of hours with the Indians to the west. When I can't get up there myself, she brings them medicine and shows them how to take it. She's also a midwife to some of the women there. They were childhood sweethearts, she and Jed. She was very wild, I'm told, when they were young. Broke a lot of hearts. Was involved in a few scandals. And was really beautiful. But then her young brother died of a cancer and it took him a long time to die and she was with him every day. I'm told she'd stay in his room twenty-four hours at a time, sometimes. And it changed her. She didn't want anything to do with any of her former ways or former friends. And that included Jed. He had some wild oats to sow anyway. And when he came back, she still didn't want to have anything to do with him. But he promised he'd changed. He took a job at the bank his father had started and settled down. She finally agreed to marry him after they'd been courting for three years."

"And then Jenny Rice killed his brother."

"If that's your opinion."

"You don't think she's guilty?"

Paul's grave was on the side of a hill overlooking the river. The air was laced with looping butterflies and soaring birds and a stray ground-sniffing dog or two. The flowers—fiercely vivid in color and scent, azaleas and roses and tulips—gave the mournful ground life and dignity. They almost made you forget about the nightcrawlers.

"I don't know either way, Bryce. But she's been a patient of mine for five years and what they say she did seems highly unlikely. She's one of the quietest, most undemonstrative women I've ever known. Except for how she treats her poor colored man, Forgarty. I think she takes all her pent-up anger out on him. I can't be around her when she's like that. But overall she's very nice. She plays the cello most of the time. She's very good at it. She lives modestly on inherited money and reads all the latest books and tends to her garden. And she works at the hospital, reading to patients and talking to them. She's even helped out with these malaria cases, before she was arrested. Now does that sound like a cold-blooded killer to you?"

"Maybe it was just impulse. She couldn't take it anymore," I suggested. "She was having an affair with him and he was leaving her for another woman."

"Has anybody ever said her name?"

"Whose name?"

"This so-called other woman. We're told there was another woman but we've never seen her. I think that's sort of strange."

"Maybe the county attorney doesn't think it's relevant to bring her to court." I had to be careful. I'd start sounding like a jailhouse lawyer.

"Maybe. But I also have a hard time believing that Jenny Rice kept a gun in her house."

"Lots of women keep guns in their houses."

"Jenny's parents were Quaker."

"People change."

"Not Jenny. Her folks—right before they passed—really pushed for the no-gun ordinance in town here. And Jenny agreed with them. You can have all the hunting guns you want but handguns you have to tell the police chief about. Just let him know you have them. For most people that's no problem. But there're a few people he won't let have any guns."

"How's Chief Pekins doing, by the way?"

"Fine. I got the bullet out. He's resting." She glanced back toward town. "I need to get back." Then, "You look sort of peaked this morning. Are you all right?"

"I'm fine," I said.

"Good. I hope you stay that way."

She turned and spent a long silent moment with him. When she left, she was crying again.

When I got back to the hotel, the desk clerk told me Krohn was looking for me. I found him on a bench in the city park. An old copy of *Police Gazette* was tented over his face to keep the sun out. I pulled his legs off the bench and sat down and lit up a cigarette.

He kept the magazine covering his face and said, "This is gonna cost you."

"How much?"

"Twenty gold dollars."

"You must've found them for that much money."

"I'm pretty sure I did."

I grabbed the magazine off his face and said, "Sit up

here, Krohn. This is my brother we're talkin' about. I don't want any coy bullshit, you understand?"

"Man, what bit you on the ass?"

"You did. My little brother's dead and I'm not in a mood for games."

He sat up. "You wouldn't have a drink on you, would you?"

"Yeah, I carry a barrel of brandy around with me. Just like a Saint Bernard."

"Never hurts to ask."

"Who are they and where are they?"

"Keep yer fuckin' pants on, Lamont. I'm gettin' to it."

"Twenty-*five* gold dollars if you get me to them."

He whistled. "You ever hear of a gang named the Waylands?"

"No."

"Neither did I. They're down from Canada."

"What the hell're they doin' down here?"

He shook his head. "Those're the boys you're lookin' for, anyway."

"How do you know all this?"

"Because the wounded one only made it as far as the state border. They had to take him to a doc and when they left him, he told the doc everything."

"How'd you find out?"

"Telegraph man's a friend of mine."

He may have been telling me something that I could've found out for free just by asking Chief Pekins. But somehow I doubted Pekins wanted me directly involved in any chase.

Canada didn't make sense. Why the hell would they come all the way down here?

"They rob anything else down here?"

"Not that the wounded one mentioned. Said they came down here just for this one."

"Wonder what the hell that's all about? This sure isn't a big enough bank for that kind of ride."

He gave me the full face of his brown, beard-ringed smile. "Maybe there was somethin' in that bank we don't know about."

"Like what?"

"Some kind of gold shipment."

"What would that be doing here?"

"Decoy. Put out all kinds of false rumors to confuse the robbers. Then they stash the gold in some podunk bank for a few weeks. Nobody except the shipper knows where it is for sure. Pretty hard for robbers to get at."

"I don't know; that doesn't sound right to me for some reason."

He shrugged. "Maybe they got kin around here. Maybe they got a grudge against somebody. Maybe they're on a spree and this is just the first bank they hit."

"Maybe, maybe, maybe."

"I'm tryin' to earn my money is all, Lamont."

I leaned back against the bench. "Where do you think they're holed up?"

"There's deep woods about thirty miles from here. A man could hide out there a long, long time before anybody caught him. If he knew what he was doin'."

"You know those woods?"

"Fair, I'd say. Long, long time ago I was a half-assed scout for some lumber people."

"You think we could find them?"

"I sure think we could try."

"I give you the money, could you put up what we need for the trip?"

"Not that much, Lamont. Couple canteens of water and some jerky and lots of ammunition."

"I'll need a rifle. A Winchester."

"No problem there."

"How long before we can leave?"

"I'd just as soon wait till morning, now."

"Not me. I don't want to give them any more of a chance than we need to."

He considered me a long silent time. "You feelin' all right?"

"Yeah. Why?"

"You don't look so good."

"Everybody around here's so concerned with my health. I've got a bit of flu or something. Nothing serious."

"You know what's goin' around. I don't have to remind you of that, do I?"

"It never happens to me. I'm one of those people who can walk through a snake pit and not get bit once." I stood up. "So, c'mon. Let's leave as soon as we can. You get everything put up."

"I'll need money."

I gave him money. I had a lot of it since Jed paid me off. I counted it out in his palm.

"You're a little short."

"Oh?"

"You give me money for provisions but nothin' for me. Twenty-five gold dollars you said. Remember?"

"Half now and half when we find them."

"Okay by me." He practically put his hand in my face. "Twelve more gold pieces, Mr. Lamont."

I gave him the additional gold pieces. He went away. I started to head back to the hotel but then exhaustion and a chill pushed me back onto the park bench.

I closed my eyes. The glands in my neck felt full and sore, the way they do with flu. And the damned chill lingered. I wanted to wrap myself in a blanket, which was ridiculous because the sun was out and it was at least seventy degrees.

There were birds and kids and pretty ladies and beautiful budding flowers and it was no time to be sick. No time to be sick at all.

TEN

I ONCE HEARD a politician say, and he seemed to be sincere, that the way the white man destroyed the Indian was actually a blessing in disguise.

"Look at these poor wretches. What do they know of real democracy? Of Shakespeare? Of vaudeville? Or of God—the one and only true God? They don't even understand that we're actually doing them a favor, killing them off the way we are. Such misery needs surcease and I say surcease it now. I wish every white man, woman, and child in this territory would pick up a rifle and do away with the first three Indians they came in contact with. If we did this once a month for a year, our Indian problem would pretty much take care of itself."

I'd always been proud to be a white man after I heard that speech. Here the way we'd been beating, cheating, whumping, burning, lynching, and shooting the Indians had actually been to their benefit. Believe it or not, the man

who said this was Oklahoma's first territorial governor, and
later went on to serve in the Senate.

I thought of all this as we started into the deepest part
of the forest, me, Krohn, and our horses. I was hoping that
the Ojibwas who still inhabited a good portion of this forest-
dense land had never heard the aforementioned politician explain his views on red-white race relations. The Indian wars
were over for the most part but you still heard, from time
to time, of skirmishes in which a small band of Indians decided to cut up a few white men. On general principle, I
could understand why they wanted to do this. I was less
generous when it became personal, with me as the cut-ee.

Krohn seemed to know what he was doing, when to
switch from one nearly invisible trail to another, when to
stop and let the animals drink of a blue, blue nearby lake,
and when to stop until a bear passed us by. No sense in
scaring them, he said.

It was out of a storybook, bars of golden sunlight stream-
ing into clearings that looked as if a human foot had never
set foot on them. Clearings and mountainlike limestone cliffs
and canoe-rivers that you could imagine prehistoric men
floating down on their rafts.

To the west and south the loggers had gone to work. I'd
seen the damage they'd done from my train window coming in. But here you could envision Eden, even God perhaps. The funny thing was the silence. There must have
been two hundred animals, insects, and rodents all making
their obstinate noises at once. And yet the scene here was
so virginal, there was only silence.

Nightfall came gradually. I kept looking at the moon take
shape in the color-shifting dusk; blue sky, gold-trimmed
clouds; salmon-pink sky, fuchsia-trimmed clouds; bloodred
sunset, thunderheads.

The rain came soon.

Krohn found us a cave. I built a fire—with him over-seeing and clucking scorn all the time I worked at it—and we had coffee and some hard rolls and some jerky. Prison food looked pretty good after this, even with all the little but mighty bugs crawling around in the soup and the por-ridge.

Neither of us talked much—just listened to the steady rain, feeling an animal gratitude for our shelter.

After a while the steady drum of the rain sounded pretty lonely and I started to think about the kid again and it got pretty bad for me. Krohn must've sensed this. He shoved his pint at me. I drained off a good bit of it. He didn't seem to mind.

An old wandering dog came in around ten o'clock, soaked and shaking. I took my blanket and wiped him off. He smelled of wet dog and there aren't many smells as spir-ited as that one.

He must have thought we were buddies. He ended up sleeping next to me. He woke me up with his dog alarm clock, his long pink tongue. A couple swipes at my face and I was wide awake.

The rain had stopped. I got the fire going again and we had morning coffee.

"We should get there by the end of the day," Krohn said as he wrapped his hands around his steaming tin mug.

"I hope so."

"You figured out what you're gonna do yet?"

"I'll see when we get there."

"You better be ready to shoot. And kill."

"That won't be any problem."

The heated anger was gone. Maybe it was the energy-draining trek through the woods. What remained was simple resolve. I wanted my brother's death avenged. I was going to give them a choice. Go back with me peacefully and take the chance of being hanged. Or have it out on the spot. At the moment, I didn't give a damn which it was.

Around noon we spotted an Ojibwa site. Birchbark wigwams built next to a river. Birchbark canoes lining the bank. The women were pounding seeds and grinding corn. They watched us pass up on the hill. They didn't wave, just watched. I waved. They still just watched.

"You ever hear of the Chipewyans?" Krohn asked me.

"Guess not."

"Distant relatives of these folks."

"You going to give me another history lesson?" I asked.

"Just a short one."

"Good. I like them."

"They eat their own. If they have to."

"The Ojibwas?"

"No. The Chipewyans."

"Man, I don't think I could ever get that hungry."

"They don't do it very often and they don't want to—I mean, it's not like some kinda celebration or nothin'—but if they have to, they will."

I just couldn't imagine it.

"I ate some human meat once."

"Aw, shit, Krohn, I don't think I want to hear about this."

"Dead of winter. Three of us. This is back in my scoutin' days. Blizzard had us pinned down in this cabin way up in the northern woods near the border. No food for three weeks. Very little water. Then this soldier boy, he gets gangrene in his leg and there ain't jack shit we can do about it and he ups and dies, see?

"So what does this colonel say? He says, we been drinking our piss to stay alive. Guess now we'll have to eat the corporal. When he said it, me'n this sergeant, we busted out laughin'. The sergeant said, 'You know I was really thinkin' about doin' it. But when you say it out loud, it sure does sound crazy, don't it?'

"So we left the corporal alone for a couple days. No chance he was gonna rot when the cabin was that cold. And then one night, he didn't even wait for us to go to sleep, the colonel just goes over there and rips off the corporal's left sleeve and saws off a piece of meat. Then he fries it up in this little pan we had. And all me'n the sarge did was watch, see? We couldn't believe the colonel was actually gonna do it. But he did it. Sprinkled salt and pepper on it. And started eatin'."

Krohn paused his horse to check out the lay of the land, then turned slightly west. "At first you could tell he was squeamish and all. And he says to hisself at one point, 'May God forgive me.' But it was kinda funny, the more he ate, the more he started to enjoy it. All this time he'd been avoidin' us, like we wasn't really there or nothin'. And then he looks at us real sudden-like and says, 'It tastes kinda like beef,' and the sarge says 'No shit, beef?' '*Just* like beef, matter of fact,' the colonel says.

"So the sarge saws hisself off a piece too. And he gives me just a teeny tiny taste of it and I'll be jiggered if it didn't taste *exactly* like beef. So later on I sawed off some of his shoulder and cooked me up some of my own. The shoulder's the best part. I mean, it ain't as tender as regular cow beef but it ain't real tough, either."

"Thanks for the dining tip."

"You'd be surprised what you're capable of sometimes."

"No, I wouldn't. And I'm afraid to know, actually. I don't like to think of myself that way."

He gave me his best brown stumpy smile. "A con man with character. Now there's something to write home about."

I reined in my horse. He did the same.

"Who told you I was a con man?"

"Stodla."

"I didn't know you knew Stodla."

"I know everybody, Lamont. Practically, anyway."

"What'd he say?"

"That you used to practice the long con. You know, swindling. Then you and Stodla got into robbing banks."

"He didn't mention Jed?"

"Jed Wylie?" He was mighty excited at the prospect of this kind of information. "He travel with you?"

"No, he didn't travel with us. But he helped bail us out a couple of times."

He looked suspicious. "That all he did?"

"That's all he did, Krohn. Take my word for it."

The smile. "A con man askin' me to take his word for it. You're just full of surprises today, ain't you, Lamont?"

Made sense for Stodla to protect Jed's reputation in a town like this. Jed wouldn't be any use to Stodla if he was seen as a bad man.

He nodded to the trail. "We got a ways to go. We'd better hit it."

We hit it. A couple of times we saw settlers chopping down trees, clearing a place for their cabin. They gave us some of their food. We didn't need any water.

The chills came back. And all at once.

I was following Krohn on the trail and then I was shaking again. They weren't dramatic chills. They didn't knock me off my animal and hurl me to the ground and start me dancing around on the grass. Not the way I'd seen some people get sick with it.

But they made me feel weak and sometimes my eyes didn't seem to focus right. I didn't say anything to Krohn. I'd seen enough of him now to know that his loyalty extended only to the dollar amount you'd given him. If he knew I was sick, he just might decide to desert. A sick man was dangerous in the kind of situation we were heading into. A sick man could get Krohn killed and Krohn wanted none of that. He was a cockroach but being a cockroach was better than being dead, at least to him.

The rains came and I was glad of it. He'd want to settle in for the rest of the day. I'd have a chance to rest tonight. Maybe I'd feel better tomorrow. Even if it was malaria, I could probably chase it away with just quinine. I wasn't anywhere near as sick as the kid had been.

We didn't find a cave but he made a kind of hut out of low-hanging fir tree boughs. He was good, quick, agile. I'd wondered about his scouting story. It sounded like barroom bragging. *Yessir, I was in them Injun wars and I fought me hand-to-hand with Geronimo hisself and I kicked that Injun around so hard he run off on me. Didn't want no part of me, I can tell you that. Them Injuns is chickenshits when you come right down to it.*

I built the fire again. I stayed close to the flames. I kept guzzling coffee, too. The heat of it warmed me. I wanted sleep. The patter of the now-light rain would put me in dreamland like a lullaby. I suppose there's a part in all of us that wants to be a little tyke again. Feel that kind of safety and snugness. During the years my parents were alive, I'd often felt it. But not after they died. I realized then that it's in the wind, death is, just waiting to light somewhere. So be ready, as the priests always tell you.

"I tell you about my kid?" Krohn asked.

"No."

"Had an Injun wife. And they had them a kid. Know where he is now?"

"Where?"

"Prison."

"I'm sorry."

"I'm not. He's where he belongs. In fact, they shoulda hung him."

I wasn't sure I'd ever heard a parent speak that way of their own child.

"What'd he do?"

"Set fire to his girlfriend's cabin. Killed her and her little sister."

"Why didn't they hang him?"

"Said he wasn't right. You know, in the head."

"You sound like you don't believe it."

"You know how them fucking lawyers is. They'll say anything." Then, "The old lady—my wife—she cut her wrists over it."

"She die?"

"She sure did. Come home one day and there she was. Sprawled on the bed. Blood everywhere. You bleed like a fucking pig, you cut your wrists that way."

"She leave a note?"

He snorted. "Yeah. 'I know he done wrong but he's the only son we got and I love him. I just can't take this no more, Krohn. I'm sorry.' " Then, "Fuckin' bitch. Killed me when she killed herself. I ain't been a fit man since. Just some kind of animal."

Cockroach, I thought.

"I don't want for nothin' but to see the next dawn. I don't give a shit who I hurt, steal from, or cheat. I truly don't."

"Because of her?"

"Her, and him," Krohn replied grimly.

"Your boy."

He didn't say anything for a time and then he said, "I went to see him once in territorial prison. He lost so much weight I didn't recognize him. He had scars on his face, too. They cut him up, I guess. And you know what I did right there in that room where everybody could see me and hear me?"

"What?"

"I started bawlin' like a baby. I never done that in my life before and I done some pretty strange things."

"How come you cried?"

"Because I knew I loved him and knew I loved her and it was all gone and dead inside me and I was helpless. Totally helpless. I was alive but I didn't want to be, but I was scared to die so all I could do was drift. And that's all I done since. Drift. I stay in town for a while and then I drift away. And come back. It's like a circle." Then, "You ever feel helpless?"

"All the time."

"Your friend's right."

"About what?"

"I don't reckon God wants us to be happy." Then, "Bet you wish I'd shut up and let you get some sleep, don't you?"

"I'm sorry it all happened to you, Krohn."

And I *was* sorry, too. I really was. For all of us who feel helpless most of the time. Because there isn't any worse way to feel.

Ten minutes later, he was snoring. And ten minutes after that, I was probably snoring, too.

I woke up a few hours later, feeling worse. I got the quinine in me and then threw a couple of Dr. Sappington's

Anti-Malarial pills down me. I had a cigarette. Every once in a while you get one that tastes so fine you know you'll never quit smoking, no matter what some of the docs'll tell you about the devil weed. In the clear midnight air under the fragrant overhang of the fir branches, that cigarette tasted and smelled damned good.

I was just about ready to give it up and lie down again when I heard the noise in the woods to my west. Whoever he was, he wasn't much good at stalking. He made as much noise as a buffalo.

If his intentions had been good, he would have used the narrow balding patch of dirt Krohn called a trail. But he was using the woods to conceal himself and that meant trouble.

I put my .45 in my hand and crawled just outside the sleeping quarters Krohn had constructed. The branches were heavy with raindrops. When I crawled underneath them, they gave me a shower. They didn't help my chills any.

I crouched beneath a fir and waited. There was a minty, clean smell on the late night air. It almost made me feel good.

He kept on making noise.

I could picture him. He'd sighted us somehow and he was going to sneak up on us. For what? He was going to be damned disappointed if he wanted to rob us. We didn't have anything worth taking. Maybe he wanted to kill us. Maybe he was one of the bank robbers who'd swung back to see if anybody had picked up their trail yet. Easy enough to shoot two men while they were sleeping. Even if you were knocking down half the trees in the woods while you were doing it.

Rustle of tree; *splat* sound of big, flat foot in muddy earth; cough of lungs getting invaded by the cold and the rain. Oh, he was some sneak thief, he was. The only thing he didn't do to attract attention was sing. And who knew, a couple of minutes, he might well break into song.

Then he was in the small clearing around our campsite. I'd never seen him before but I'd sure seen his type plenty of places. He was straight out of a dime novel. He had your ten-gallon hat. He had your hip-slung holster. He had your fancy neckerchief. He had your even fancier leather vest and your dark western shirt with the white piping. The kid belonged on a stage, not out here in these godforsaken woods.

I said, "Drop the gun."

He came apart. Literally. His limbs started jerking and angling and fixing themselves into impossible positions as he tried to unify his body parts into a coordinated and coherent physical response to my voice. All the fancy duds in the world weren't doing him any good now.

"You gonna shoot me? My name's Carmody. I don't mean you no harm, mister. I really don't."

"Who the fuck is this?" Krohn said, waking up, gawking at our intruder.

"I'm gonna shoot you if you don't drop that gun."

Krohn said, "Lamont? Where the hell are you?"

"There's a reward on your head, mister," Carmody said.

"Did you hear what I said about the gun?" I asked.

"You'd really shoot me?"

"Of course, I'd really shoot you, you dumb shit. I'm a bad man."

"Lamont, what the hell is going on here?" Krohn asked one more time.

"I'm going to shoot this dumb asshole," I finally replied.

"Shoot him? Who the hell is he?"

"I imagine he thinks he's a bounty hunter."

"Mr. Jed Wylie, he put a two-thousand-dollar reward on your heads,"

Krohn said, "You stupid bastard. You think we're the bank robbers?"

"I sure do, mister."

"Lamont, I can't even see you. But will you go ahead and shoot this ignorant sonofabitch?"

"It'll be my pleasure."

"No—wait. You really gonna shoot?" Carmody asked one more time.

"Yeah, he's really gonna shoot. Ain't you, Lamont?"

"I sure am."

"Then I'm droppin' my gun. It ain't worth dyin' for."

"Throw that gun over here," Krohn said. "Stupid fucker." Then, "Lamont, you know how old this idiot is?"

"Maybe sixteen."

"Sixteen, hell. I'm bettin' no more than fourteen. Right, kid?"

"I'm fifteen."

Krohn said, "Fifteen and you don't know jack shit."

"I don't?"

"Are you in the union?"

"What union?"

"You hear that, Lamont? This stupid asshole wants to know what union. The bounty hunters' union, of course."

"They have a union?" Carmody asked.

"You're damn right they do."

"And a secret handshake, too," I said.

"Aw, bullshit," the kid said.

"Well, at least he ain't *that* dumb." Krohn laughed.

He then walked right up to the kid, kneed him in the groin, seized his throat, and started choking him one-handed until the kid was gagging and flailing around for air, then hit him so hard in the stomach that the kid started puking all over himself. Then Krohn pushed him to the ground.

Raindrop-soaked, I came out from under the trees.

"You didn't tell me nothin' about no secret handshake," Krohn said.

"You gotta start comin' to meetings more often."

But our high hilarity was wasted on the kid. He was too busy being sick.

Krohn put on coffee. I changed into a dry shirt and put on my denim jacket.

When we got him sitting next to the fire, the kid said, "Only reason I done it is 'cause they's gonna take the farm back."

"What farm?" I asked.

"My pa's."

"Who's takin' it back?" Krohn asked.

"Mr. Wylie's bank."

"Why would he take it back?" I asked again.

"Pa ain't made no payments for more'n two years."

"How come?"

"Broke his back when he fell out of the haymow. He had cowshit all over his shoes and it was slippery and he just fell over backward off'n that ladder. The cows was real sick and their shit was really runny."

"Kid, we ain't the bank robbers," I reassured Carmody.

"Bullshit."

Krohn rolled his eyes. "Kid, we're *after* the bank robbers."

He looked at me, then back to Krohn. "No bullshit?"

"No bullshit," I said.

"Aw, fuck."

"What?" I said.

"Well, if'n I have to split that money three ways, I won't have enough to pay off the bank."

Krohn and I smiled at each other. We could just see this hayseed sauntering into the house where the robbers were holed up. He'd be dead in thirty seconds—after he gave them all a couple of good laughs.

"Where'd you git them clothes?" Krohn said.

"My older brother was in this here pageant one time for Governor's Day and they let him keep the duds. Why? I think they're kinda sharp."

"Yeah, kid," Krohn said, "that's just what they are. Sharp."

"I'm freezin'," the kid said.

Krohn finished his coffee then filled the cup up for the kid and handed it to him.

"The chief, he ain't far behind me," Carmody said.

"How many hours you reckon?" Krohn asked.

"Three. Four, maybe."

"You think he camped for the night?"

"I was on a hill a while back. I seen a fire."

"How come he took so long to git goin'?" Krohn asked.

"Arm's givin' him trouble. Where he was shot, I mean. Took him a while to feel strong enough to ride."

We'd bought all the time we were going to get. Somebody had given Pekins the same information Krohn had given me. At most I'd get an hour or two alone with the robbers. That was, if I could figure out a way to get in there in the first place.

"Go home, kid," I said.

"What?" I'd startled him.

"Go home."

"Why?"

"Because you're going to get killed."

Krohn said, "He's right. Everybody shows up where they are tomorrow, there's gonna be so much gunfire, a lot of people'll die for no good reason at all."

"I ain't afraid," the kid said, puffing out his skinny chest.

"That's part of the problem, kid," Krohn said. "You're too *stupid* to be afraid. And it's that kinda thing that's gonna get you killed."

He'd hurt the kid's feelings. "Quit sayin' I'm stupid. I ain't stupid. I'm just tryin' to help out my pa. "

I said, "Tell you what, kid. You go on home. We'll beat Pekins and his men to the robbers. Then we'll get the reward and we'll turn it over to you."

"You serious?"

"Bullshit, we will," Krohn said.

"You're my employee, Mr. Krohn," I said. "I learned enough jailhouse law to know that you're not entitled to anything we accrue on this trip, up to and including a reward. That will go directly and completely to me. To be disposed of as I see fucking fit. Do you understand me, Mr. Krohn?"

"This is really bullshit."

"You'd really give it to me?" the kid asked again.

"If you go back to town at dawn, I will."

"Gosh. That's really great of you."

"Me'n you's gonna have us a talk," Krohn said to me. "A nice, long one."

ELEVEN

ABOUT EVERY TWENTY minutes, Krohn'd get mad all over again. "You didn't have no right to do that."

"I had every right," I told him.

"Half that reward money's mine."

"Not according to the law, it isn't."

"Fuck the law."

"Yeah, you say that to a judge and see what happens."

He'd sulk silently for a while as we followed another one of what he called his "Injun" trails. The medicines I'd taken seemed to've helped some. I didn't feel great but I didn't feel too bad, either.

"Over this hill and down in a valley," he said as the sun reached noon in the blue prairie sky, "there's a deserted stage stop. That's one of the places they might be holed up."

"I don't want to wait till night."

"Won't have to. There's a creek runs behind it. Steep banks. We can crawl along there till we're right in back of the place. If they're there, we ain't gonna see no horses. They're probably in the woods."

"So we go in shooting?"

He smiled. "You're as green as that damned kid about stuff like this, ain't you?"

"I've never killed anybody before. I guess I just walk in and do it, huh?"

The smile he gave me this second time was not unkind. "Lamont, the one that killed your brother is already dead. I doubt the other men wanted anybody killed. That just makes things worse for them. So you get inside and you see these three outlaws. Now which one you gonna hold accountable for your brother's death?"

"All of them."

"All right. That's fair enough. So which ones you gonna shoot?"

"All of them."

"Well, like you said, you never killed nobody before."

"So?"

"So it's different once you do. Once you go over and really *look* at what you done. He was a whole little world, a whole history. He had kin who loved him and respected him and who needed him. To you he wasn't nothin' but a fuckin' outlaw. But he was other things, too, other things you can't afford to think about because if you *did* think about 'em you probably wouldn't be able to kill him."

"You sound like a priest."

"I was in a county jail once with this priest. I guess he must've taught me a lot. I ain't killed a man since."

"What was the priest doin' in jail?"

"He was a cocaine addict. He let everything around him go to shit just so he could keep his habit goin'. Finally got so bad he started breakin' into the houses of people he was givin' communion to every day, if you can figure that. He hung hisself one night; shit his pants harder'n any man I ever saw. Shit runnin' down his legs and shoes. And the stink was somethin', too."

I said, "Well, I can kill them."

"If you say so."

"You just wait till we get there."

This time the smile was cold, wise in a hard way. "Guess that's about all I *can* do, isn't it, Lamont? Just wait and see how you act once we get there."

We climbed the hill. The shacklike ranch house below us looked shabby and deserted, as if all life had moved on from it. Usually, a place like this, you'd see animals scampering around. But there was nothing here. Nothing at all.

"You think somebody's down there?"

Krohn said, "Can't tell."

"The creek?"

"Looks like. We'll swing over to the east. Pick it up there."

"You like bein' the boss, Krohn?"

"Yessir"—he laughed—"I like it just fine."

The ride was longer than it looked. We ground-tied our mounts behind a windbreak of oaks and then started down the forty-five-degree slant of the creek bank. Creek was almost a misnomer. It was ten foot wide and fast running. A milk snake on a rock watched us with avid disinterest. A crow paused long enough from eating a dead fish to give us his black-eyed disapproval. A hawk soared low overhead, seeing what was going on.

We had our guns drawn. We walked bent over, like old arthritic men. Every ten feet or so, Krohn signaled to stop. He'd cock his head and listen. I never heard anything. Apparently, he didn't either.

The water smelled in places. The funny thing was that you couldn't see anything wrong. No dead animals, no human waste, no other kind of corrupted material floating down the creek. But you sure could smell it. Industrial dumping was becoming a problem in places. There'd been a big battle in an Iowa border town over a tannery that had dumped so many chemicals in the water, the whole leg of the river turned red.

Krohn whispered, "We're just about there."

"How do you know?"

The bank was too tall to see over. How could Krohn know where we were relative to the stage stop without climbing up the bank and looking?

"I just know things like that."

I smiled. "I guess I'll have to take your word for it."

"Just because I'm a drunk don't mean I'm stupid."

"No, but it doesn't help any, either."

We went another ten yards and then he stopped. "It's right up there."

"The stage stop?"

"You bet."

"You mind if I peek first?"

"I'll peek. You'll just get your head blowed off."

So he finger-dug his way up the muddy bank and said, "Shit."

"Not up there, is it?"

"'Bout another tenth of a mile down."

We went the rest of the way in silence.

When we reached the waist-high grass between creek and stage stop, we crouched down and fanned out. I half-expected to be shot at any moment. Easy to imagine somebody with a rifle following me from some window. Then

killing me soon as I drew close enough. The danger was
enough to make me forget my malaria.

The buildings consisted of a wind-smashed barn, an outhouse, an empty corral, and a two-story frame house. Most
of the windows had been smashed out. The place looked
long deserted. The wind made a whistling sound racing
around the rooms on the second floor.

I knew enough to look for fresh horse tracks. There were
none I could see. Krohn was probably right. They would've
hid their mounts in the woods.

I still had the sense I was being watched. The gun trembled slightly in my hand. I crouched at the edge of the long
grass. A few inches away was the back yard, which was
mostly plain dirt. I checked out each window individually,
trying to account for the sense I was being watched. But
the windows, so far as I could see, were empty.

Then Krohn was there, crouching next to me.

"You see anything?" he whispered.

"Nothing."

"Me, neither. But it still could be a trap."

"How?"

"They could be waiting for us inside."

"You get the feeling somebody's got a rifle trained on
us?"

The brown grin. "I was *born* feelin' like that, Lamont."

"So now we go in?"

"Now we go in."

"You ready?"

I nodded.

He stood up, which surprised me.

He saw me hesitate. "Hell, if they're in there, they're
gonna pick us off anyway, whether we're crouched down
or walkin' regular."

I stood up. We walked toward the house. The back porch door came off its lone hinge when I put my hand on the knob. It fell dustily backward.

"Well," Krohn said, "if they didn't know we were here, they sure do now."

We went inside. The kitchen was a mess, a bloody mess. A bunch of animals—looked to be squirrels—had been slaughtered for eating. You could see heads and tails and dried-up innards all over. Everything stank of blood. There was an ancient calendar from a funeral home on the wall: 1879.

There was no furniture anyway. Just droppings from just about every animal you could think of except for an elephant maybe. Our boots made a lot of noise crunching through all that dried dung.

The upstairs bedroom still smelled faintly of perfume. It was funny, after all these years, that a scent like that would linger. It wasn't strong, as I said, but it was there, like the forgotten words of lovers carried back on the wind.

There was no trim on the rooms. They were bare of everything but cheap paint sloppily applied. The floor was freckled with dozens of paint droppings. There was the sour stench of long-ago chamber pots. A tiny mouse peered out at me from a hole in the far wall. The way he worked his whiskers was cute. I wondered what he'd do all day long in a place like this. No food. No life.

I found cigarette butts, an empty pint of rotgut, and a shirt soaked with blood in a tiny attic. This is where they'd holed up for the night after killing the squirrels. The attic was empty, dusty. I had to squat to walk around. Rat turds were everywhere, along with some kind of invisible but choking dust. I found a kerchief that was also blood-soaked. There was a good chance the robber had been wounded more seriously than we'd thought. Maybe he was dead by now. Maybe we'd only be facing two of them when we caught up with them.

What appeared to be a spare room—probably a spare bedroom in case the number of guests had grown too large for the stop to handle comfortably—was on the east side of the house. There were sprinklings of tobacco on the floor, the pieces fresh and moist; there was an empty box for .45 shells, which also looked new; and there were boot scrapes on the dust-lined floor, raw and new.

They'd been here all right.

Probably posted a guard in this room because it gave them the best view of the yard and the surrounding countryside.

Krohn was in the doorway.

"They were here, huh?"

"Sure looks that way. They're long gone, though." I told him about the bloody shirt and kerchief.

"He might be dead."

"I like the idea of that just fine. Guess we might as well push on," I said. "They aren't here."

"Not necessarily."

"What?"

"This could be a trick."

"What the hell're you talkin' about?"

"Heard us coming. Snuck out and waited for us in the woods to the west. An old Indian trick. Lure the soldiers into a camp that looked deserted."

"You speaking from experience?"

"You damned bet I am."

We spent twenty minutes more searching the house and the grounds. Nothing. Even Krohn came to accept the fact that they were gone.

We rode. According to him, there was a small ghost town six to seven miles to the west. The trail was good so we could ride into the night. If I felt up to it. I told him my fever had broken and I was feeling stronger. He said good.

He told me about the ghost town. Railroad had made a deal with a couple of investors. Put up a town at such and such a location and we'll make sure you're on the rail route.

The investors, who'd run into some bad luck with other projects, put everything they had into the rail spur. They were finally going to be rich. This was what America was all about. Just ask old John D. Rockefeller. He wasn't afraid to say what was in the back of everybody's mind: If an American wasn't rich, it meant that he'd done something wrong, committed some secret sin so grievous God wouldn't allow him the right to be wealthy.

What they hadn't counted on, these hapless investors, was the railroad itself going bust. But it did. There were short-line operators all over the place going broke. The big operators were running them out of business by starting freight price wars in every sector of the country. No short line could compete against the prices the big boys were offering.

They'd set up a skeleton town. They'd invited the governor. They'd laid in hootch and gals and even a couple of professional speakers from Chicago to make with the fancy words . . . and then, three days before it was all supposed to come true, the short line was forced into bankruptcy.

They then tried to auction the town off to the highest bidder. But who wanted a town out here near nothing? They tried to give it away to the state government but it seemed the "town" had already accrued some tax debt and some fine debt for not securing proper permits, etc., and fucking etc.

They fled, the town fathers. What the hell else could they do? They didn't have two dollars between them, their greed had led them to be laughingstocks, and their troubles with the state government told them that there were even more problems ahead.

So they fled. And who could blame them?

This was the town we were headed toward as night crept gently across the sky, bringing with it the song of nightbirds and the lonely cries of coyotes and wild dogs, and the fresh scents of a spring night.

There were two facing half-blocks of false-fronts. Faded signs read POST OFFICE, SALOON, GENERAL MERCHANDISE, BLACKSMITH, and so on. There were hitching posts and watering troughs and two poles for telegraphs. Everything looked as if it had been put together cheaply and hastily. There was no pride here. I saw all this through my field glasses. At eleven P.M., the dead little town was in deep shadow, not even the bright moon and starry sky able to give it the glow of life. The town was in a small valley surrounded by pine trees. You could smell a river in the distance. It was May but it felt, right now, like early March. You could see the silver skin of ice on some of the puddles.

There was a dog, a cat, and a rat. A piece of white paper got blown down the street by the wind. A second dog squatted in the center of the dusty street, emptying his bowels. Somewhere a loose shutter banged.

Krohn had his own field glasses.

I spent a long time searching for horse tracks in the sandy street. Didn't see any. But then the wind and the sand might have taken care of them by now. Saw no evidence of lanterns anyplace, no evidence of horse or human.

It was like a giant toy for children, the ghost town. Not

a fancy or expensive one, either. The crudeness of the construction made me wonder if the railroad hadn't done everybody a favor by folding.

Krohn said, "They're in there."

"You see them?"

"Nope. But I can feel them."

"You sure?"

"Real sure."

He dropped down off his mount, took his rifle from its scabbard. "C'mon, Lamont. Let's get it over with."

"What're we gonna do?"

Even in the dark his brown-stub smile was disgusting. "I'm gonna walk down the middle of the street and draw fire and you're gonna follow their gunfire and figure out where they're hidin'."

"What happens if you get hit?"

"That'll be my problem. You just circle wide and get in behind 'em and kill 'em. That's all you need to worry about." The smile. "If you've got it in you to kill 'em, that is."

"I got it in me. They killed my brother."

"That don't mean jack shit, Lamont. Not when you're thinkin' about actually takin' somebody else's life. All this dime-novel bullshit you read about men shootin' other men all the time, most of it ain't true and the part of it that *is* true is about mad dogs. And the Lord be praised, there ain't many of them. Or we wouldn't have no civilization at all. You ain't no mad dog, Lamont. So I still ain't sure you can do it."

"I guess we'll find out soon enough."

I was climbing down out of the saddle when I passed out. It came pretty fast. The sickness had been acting up again, then it overwhelmed me. I fell straight out of the saddle and right down onto the ground, slamming my head hard when I landed.

The next thing I saw was Krohn leaning over me. "You're gettin' hot."

"Hot?"

"Your fever. You musta passed out."

"Guess I did." I had a pretty bad headache. When I tried to sit up, it just got worse.

"Stay down awhile."

"I want to get in there."

"You ain't gonna do nobody no good the way you are now. You need to rest up for a while."

He dragged me over to a tree, propped me up against its base. Then he went and got the canteen. The water was cool and good. I closed my eyes. I don't know if I slept exactly but suddenly everything went away—the forest sounds, the starry sky, the chill hard ground. The kid and I were back on the farm playing baseball. I was throwing him softies so he'd be sure and belt it hard. Some smart boy at school said Paul swung the bat like a girl. I wanted to make sure Paul knew that wasn't true. He belted six, seven home runs. He was grinning all the time. There were other dreams too—I think Laura Westcott was in one of them—but I didn't take them back with me when I reached the real world again.

Krohn said, "Welcome back, Lamont."

"How long I been out?"

"A good hour."

"Damn."

"You got to have that lady doctor check you out. You're sicker than you think you are."

"I still want to go in there."

The brown grin. "Ain't you I'm worried about. It's me. You're supposed to be my backup."

"I'll be all right."

But as I started to stand up, I realized Krohn was right. I was still weak. Damned weak. The fever had broken but I had little energy and a smashing headache. I fell back against the tree. "Shit."

"I'll go."

Krohn and I turned around at the same time. It was Carmody, the one who wanted the reward for capturing the bank robbers, the one we'd sent back home.

"What the hell you doin' here?" Krohn said. "We told ya to go on home."

"I just got to thinkin', is all," Carmody said.

"He just got to thinkin'," Krohn said to me.

"That Mr. Lamont here is sick and all."

"Not so sick I can't do my job," I said.

"Well, just in case," Carmody said. "Just in case, is what I was thinkin'."

"Just in case what?" Krohn snapped.

"Well, just in case Mr. Lamont, he *couldn't* do the job, then you'd have me as a backup."

"Lucky us," Krohn said.

"So looks like it's pretty good timin'."

"You stupid bastard," Krohn said. "We told you to git on home."

"I don't see what yer so mad about," Carmody said.

"I'm mad because yer right."

"I am?"

"Lamont here's gonna try'n bullshit me into lettin' him be my backup. But he's too weak. Hell, he can't even stand up. But he wasn't all that good a backup anyway. He never killed a man. So now I get you, huh?"

"I want that reward, Mr. Krohn. And I want to earn it. I don't want you to just give it to me."

"You ever killed a man?"

"I held my dog Sam when he was dyin'."

"He held his dog," Krohn said, shaking his head. He looked at both of us. "I got two virgins here. Least Carmody's got an excuse. He's just some dumb prairie kid. But you shoulda killed a dozen men by now, Lamont."

"I'll work harder at that."

He stood up, knees cracking.

"All right, Junior. Looks like you're gonna be my backup."

The kid touched his holster. "You won't be sorry."

"I'm sorry already," Krohn said. "It's just there ain't a damn thing I can do about it."

Krohn spent the next ten minutes going over everything for Carmody. How he, Krohn, was going to stroll down the street and attract fire. Because surely if they were in there, they'd open up on him. And meanwhile, Carmody was gonna follow the fire, locate the robbers, and then kill them.

"In cold blood, huh?"

"In cold blood," Krohn said, "otherwise they're gonna kill you."

"I don't give them no warning?"

"No warning, kid. They're wanted for murder. We know it's them. I ain't sayin' it's the prettiest way to do it—nor the Lord's way either—but once they know you're there, they'll both turn on you and you'll be dead. I'll get there to help you as soon as I can. But they'll still have plenty of time to shoot you. So, you shoot them first."

"In the back?"

"In the back is right, kid. In the back."

"You ever shot a man in the back, Mr. Krohn?"

"When the occasion called for it."

The kid sighed. "You ever seen one of them Wild West shows?"

"Couple of times."

"They always talk about the Code of the West. You know, how a good and true man never cheats or steals or back-shoots."

"They're all a bunch of nancies."

"They are?"

"Sure. That's all bullshit, kid."

"There ain't no Code of the West?"

Krohn laughed. "Yeah, and it's do unto others before they do unto you."

Carmody laughed uneasily.

They stood up in the moonlight.

You could see that Carmody was wound tight. But so was Krohn. He kept slapping his holster as if to make sure it hadn't run away. Slapping his holster and licking his lips as if he had a badly parched throat. I didn't blame him for being scared. He was offering himself up as a target.

"You remember what to do?" Krohn said to him.

"Uh-huh."

"You sure?"

"Uh-huh."

"You check your gun?"

"Uh-huh."

"It's ready to fire?"

"Uh-huh."

I think Carmody was so scared he couldn't say anything more than "uh-huh."

"You ready?"

"Uh-huh."

"You rest up," Krohn said to me.

I nodded. It took about all the energy I had.

"He's sure got guts," Carmody said as Krohn started walking toward the town.

I nodded.

He said, "So you never killed nobody either, huh?"

"Nope," I managed to say.

"My brother killed a colored man once over a card game. He felt pretty bad about it, even though he was colored and all."

He took his gun out. He was shaking. His arms. "Guess I better get goin'." Then, "I can do it if I need to. I know I can."

He looked at me. "Kinda lucky you're sick and all." Then, "I don't mean nothin' by that."

I nodded at him again.

He went away.

The shots didn't come for a while. And then there were just two of them. Two quick shots and then nothing. As if they were waiting till he got into better range or something.

I went out again. You know how it is when you're that sick. How you fade in and out and have these quick dreams. You wake up and you're not sure if they didn't actually happen and weren't dreams at all. I was canoeing with Paul. It was on this fast gray river that ran just north of our farm. Water always scared Paul. We had a cousin who drowned. Paul saw him when they pulled him out hours later. I guess he never forgot it.

Then there were two more shots. Forty-fives, they sounded like. Colts. Then came the sounds of the Winchester. That would likely be Krohn responding. Then nothing again.

They were there, all right. We'd probably surprised them but they sure weren't going to be surprised anymore. They had the advantage of a good, secure hiding place and they were going to use it.

I wondered how Carmody was doing.

The poor kid. He reminded me of Paul in a way, that same kind of earnest innocence.

And then I started feeling better. That teeter-tottering of strength and weakness that comes with malaria sometimes. At least according to Laura Westcott. I thought of her for a good long time lying there. She was very vivid in my mind, like a religious vision, the way saints are said to appear to believers from time to time. I couldn't help the way I felt about her. I knew it wasn't right, her and Paul being what they'd been and all, but I couldn't help it.

Shouts. Gunfire. Glass breaking, windows probably. More shouts. Darkness.

I forced myself to my feet.

I came up in stages.

When I got on my feet I put my hands flat on the wet grass and pushed myself erect. I almost wobbled over backward.

Night sounds: owl, distant train, creek, and raccoons fighting over some forest treasure. I couldn't see anything in the copse of trees where we tied up our mounts.

I forced my legs to move. At first I thought I was going to pass out again. The dizziness was the worst part of it. I thought I might throw up.

But little by little, strength filled my legs, gave them direction and purpose. I even had enough stamina to slide my .45 from my holster.

After a few minutes, I was walking fine. I didn't need to lean against the trees as I walked.

Three quick shots. Revolvers.

Why wasn't Krohn firing?

And then Krohn *was* firing. Two shots.

The robbers would be in one of the buildings. So where was Krohn and where was Carmody?

Silence again.

I moved into town. The empty buildings lent the night a certain eeriness, like those ghost towns you hear about that had supposedly been routed by demons, nothing left but the bones of some former residents and strange markings on the walls.

By now, I was walking almost normally. The fever cut down on most of my senses—neither my eyes, ears, or nose were as sharp as they normally were—but I could maneuver well enough to position myself behind the false-fronts.

I kept flat to the backs of the buildings. Any further away from there, I'd probably be seen.

I listened for any sound inside.

They knew what they were doing. They didn't make a damned sound.

The sweat was starting up again. My whole chest was soaked. I had to keep wiping my gun hand off on my trousers.

And then the shot.

There was something different about this one. Maybe that was just my fever playing games with my head. But this one didn't have the same timbre as the others.

This was the one that made Krohn cry out.

I could also hear him fall on one of the board sidewalks. He'd probably been shooting from the shadows across the street when they got him.

"Finish him!" a voice called.

I hurried around the way I'd come so I could peek from behind the edge of the first building and see what was going on.

In the moonlight, I saw Krohn lying facedown, half on the boardwalk and half in the street. His whole body was bloody. He wasn't moving.

Four shots came from across the street, every one of them hitting him in the back. If he hadn't been dead before, he sure was now. He didn't move. Not once. Or make any kind of sound. He just lay there and absorbed the bullets.

I thought of Paul.

The shots were coming from the saloon. Was Carmody in there with them by now?

But I couldn't worry about Carmody now. I had to get inside the saloon myself.

I swung to the back of the buildings again, stayed in the long, inky shadows.

There was the sound of a coyote. And then an owl.

Clouds covered the half-moon.

I got to the back door of the place and stopped.

There were two ways in. A back door. And a second floor. Empty kegs were lined along the rear wall. Without too much trouble I could put one on top of the other and reach a second-floor window.

The trouble was that that would take all my strength. While I felt better, I knew I had to marshal my stamina. It wouldn't last long and I couldn't waste it.

The back door it was.

There was a lock but a cheap one. A pocketknife got it open. All I could hope was that the distance between the back door and the front windows was enough to muffle any sounds I made.

Blackness. Smell of skunky beer. Cigars.

I groped through the shadows.

Stairs—three steps. I went up them carefully, one at a time.

Another door. Not locked. I put my ear to it.

Voices, whispers really. They had to be wondering if Krohn had been the only one.

I had just put my hand on the doorknob when I heard Carmody say, "Turn around and put your guns down and don't think I don't mean it."

He sounded about ten years old. The poor kid.

"Who the hell're you?" one of them snapped.

"Don't matter who I am. Only matters who *you* two are. You're the ones who robbed the bank and killed Paul Lamont."

"Killed who?" the other one said. "We didn't kill nobody."

"Well, your friend sure did. And the kid was sick with malaria to boot, the one he shot."

"Goddamn Hardy. He musta killed somebody."

"Fuckin' idiot. I warned you about him, didn't I?" Then, "Where's Hardy?"

"That the one who shot him?"

"Yeah."

"He's dead. One of the deputies got him."

The kid was letting them get away from him. I'm sure the robbers were interested in what had happened to their friend Hardy but they were also talking the kid out of his concentration. From what I could hear, he hadn't yet gotten them to set their guns down. And there were two of them.

The kid tried to get it back.

"Set your guns down on that table over there. And don't think I won't shoot you, 'cause I will."

"How the hell old are you, kid?"

"Old enough."

"You hear that?" one of them laughed. "Old enough."

"You heard me, now. Put those guns down."

"And supposin' we don't?"

"Then I shoot you."

"Yeah. Well, I guess you'll have to go ahead and shoot us, 'cause we ain't settin' them down, are we, Frank?"

"We sure as hell ain't."

"You have to." He sounded ten years old again.

"Why?"

"Because I got the drop on you."

"You maybe got the drop on us, kid, but we're facin' you and we both got guns in our hands. Now, you can probably pick one of us off but you're gonna die doin' it, you understand?"

"This ain't the way it's supposed to be," Carmody said petulantly.

"Well, now, I couldn't tell you the way it was *supposed* to be but I can sure as hell tell you the way it is, right, Frank?"

"Right, Duffy."

"And the way it is, you got two real pissed-off gunnies in front o' you who're just itchin' to kill you just the way we killed your friend out there. You hear all the shots we pumped into that old boy?"

"Yeah, I heard all right."

"Well, sir, if I was a bettin' man, I'd say that's gonna happen to you any minute here. Wouldn't you, Frank?"

"I sure would."

"So you just go ahead and shoot, kid, and whichever one of us goes down first—t'other one'll kill you."

Frank laughed. "He's shittin his pants."

Duffy said, "I can smell it from here."

"Dumb fuckin' kid."

"Well, that ain't the way it's *supposed* to be," Duffy said mockingly.

"Dumb fuckin' kid," Frank said again.

"He sure is, ain't he?"

It was a lot longer way from the back room to the front than I realized. There were also all kinds of little traps—chairs, tables, boxes, pieces of broken glass, holes in the floor—any one of which could give me away if I nudged them or stepped on them.

I moved in a crouch, going up behind the bar so that when I finally stood up at the far end I'd be right next to Carmody.

I had to move fast because I knew that any moment now, Duffy or Frank would open fire.

And that was when I kicked the bottle that lay unseen on the floor. It was a pretty good kick. It must have rolled several feet behind the bar then slammed into the wall.

Everybody started shooting.

I killed my first man without ever thinking about it. I just fired. I fired till the gun was empty and then one of them, Duffy or Frank, I wasn't sure, just dropped. There was a lot of smoke and a lot of gunfire and a lot of cursing and screaming.

Then the other one fell.

Carmody was still standing.

I came out from behind the bar and he said, "I'll be damned, Lamont. We killed 'em."

I looked over at the two men on the floor and said, "Yeah. Yeah, I guess we did." I fumbled with my gun, opened the bullet chamber, and loaded it again, just in case.

"And it wasn't so bad. It was easy."

I showed him my hand. It was trembling. "Not that easy."

"Maybe that's your malaria."

"It isn't malaria. It's nerves."

"Poor damn Krohn."

"Yeah."

I went over and looked at them. I was half-expecting to start thinking of them as human beings, the way Krohn predicted I would. But I didn't. They were just two slabs of human meat, nothing more, nothing less. The flies were on them already. They hadn't actually pulled the trigger but if they hadn't robbed the bank, Paul would still be alive. So would Krohn, for that matter.

I was turning away from them when it happened.

"Lamont! Watch out!"

Whatever it was, all I could do was pitch myself across the bar. And as I did so I saw one of the two robbers raise up. His gun was in his hand. He'd apparently meant to fire at me but I'd thrown myself out of his path so now he aimed at Carmody.

And Carmody, who was no fast draw, was having a hell of a time getting his gun out of his holster.

Frank or Duffy got him two or three times in the chest.

By this time, I'd pitched myself off the bar top. I crawled down to the end of the bar, leaned around the corner. I had a perfect shot. I sliced a good chunk of his head away.

I hurried over to Carmody. There wasn't any hope.

I got him a shot of whiskey from behind the bar.

"I can't hold my liquor," he said. Then he smiled sadly, realizing what he'd just said. "But I guess it don't make no never mind now, does it?"

"Drink it down."

I had him propped up against the bottom of the bar. He looked young and scared and pale in the moonlight.

"You believe in heaven?" he said.

I knew what he wanted me to say. "I sure do." I smiled. "There's gotta be someplace better than this."

"Yeah. There's just gotta, don't there?"

I wasn't sure exactly when he passed. It wasn't anything dramatic. He just passed was all.

The last twenty minutes, I hadn't been aware of my illness. Too much going on. But now I could feel the fever start to build slowly, and little icy tremors just under my skin.

I took off my shirt and mopped my face. I lay back against the bar, right next to where Carmody was slumped dead. I was the only one left to get the reward. I planned to give it to his old man. That way there'd be at least some purpose to Carmody dying.

I tried to stay awake but it was impossible. Fatigue cramped my legs and arms; the buzzing headache came back. I lost my will to fight. It'd be better in the blackness.

I slept.

There was sunlight angling through the dusty front window of the saloon. Somebody was kicking the bottom of my boot.

Pekins, the chief of police. "This looks like a graveyard. Geez, the Carmody kid came after them. I didn't think he'd make it here."

"You see Krohn?"

"Saw him all right. Looks like they emptied a couple of rifles in him."

"They were sweet boys."

"Their papers say Canada."

"You don't think that's strange?"

"I'm a law officer. I think everything's strange unless you can show me otherwise. I think *you're* strange for getting involved."

"They killed my brother."

"No, they didn't. The one back at the hotel did."

"If they hadn't robbed the bank, Paul'd still be alive."

He hefted his rifle. "Guess I didn't think about it that way." He put his one good arm out. The other one was in a sling from the wound.

He helped me up. I was wobbly.

I went behind the bar and poured myself a shot.

"Little early for that, isn't it?"

"Not when you feel as bad as I do," I said.

The robbers had brought a bottle along with them. The other bottles collected above the bar were strictly for show, dusty and empty. I took a good swig.

"You need bed rest is what you need."

"I know. And I'm not gonna argue."

"We'll throw the bodies across horses and then we'll all go back to town. It's all done now."

"I get the reward, don't I?"

"Yeah."

I told him about Carmody's ranch.

He looked at me. "That's quite a gesture from a man like you."

"Is that a compliment or an insult?"

"Both."

We went outside. The sun was strong but I couldn't appreciate its blessings. You kind of crawl inside yourself when you're running a fever the way I was. You can't appreciate much at all.

"You gonna run a check on them?" I said.

"What kinda check?"

"See who they were, where they came from."

"We know who they were and where they came from."

"I'd like to see where they've spent the last five, six years or so."

"Canada."

"Maybe not. You could telegraph the law of the town where they operated out of. He could tell you some things."

He looked at me. "What crawled up your ass?"

"I'm just curious is all. All the way down from Canada. Why? It doesn't make sense to me."

"You're saying I'm not doin' my job proper-like, is what you're sayin', Mr. Lamont."

He was short, slight and his face was too boyish for the gray hair showing on the sides of his head. All of which meant that he'd probably never been taken too seriously as a lawman and thus got real tight when it seemed you were calling his competence into question.

I said, "You may have saved my life coming along when you did, Pekins. Why would I draw down on you after you did something like that? I'm just naturally curious about their coming down from Canada is all, and for not a lot of money. That's all I'm saying."

He looked at me again. This time it was a very careful appraisal. He was looking for any hint of a smirk or smile that would betray my real feelings. The thing was, those were my real feelings. He appeared to be a damned competent lawman, he truly had helped save my life, and I was genuinely curious about why a second-rate gang of Canadian banditos would heist a Wisconsin bank.

He said, quietly, "Maybe you're right, Lamont. Maybe I should send them a telegraph up there."

He didn't speak to me once on the ride back to town.

TWELVE

I GOT SICK twice more before we got back to town. At one point my fever was so high, I was delirious. Pekins and his three deputies cinched my wrists to the saddle horn so I wouldn't fall off.

I don't remember being brought up to my room.

I know they say that malarial spasms last only a couple of hours. But I guess I must've been pretty well drained of all my strength because I slept for nearly twenty-four hours.

When I woke up it was night and I thought right away of Paul. And I got sad and scared. The night seemed so big in my little room. Bad things were going to happen. I could sense them. Maybe I would've left town, I was so scared at what I felt coming down the road for me. But I was too weak.

I slept some more.

In the morning, I woke up to a cool hand on my forehead and when I looked up I saw Laura Westcott.

She helped me sit up and she gave me two different kinds of medicine. The taste of quinine was unmistakable.

"You've been a busy man."

"Yeah."

She said, "Then it's over."

"I guess."

She said, "You mean it isn't over?"

"I think it is."

"The robbers are dead."

"Yeah."

"And they recovered about half the money."

The money. I'd been so obsessed with Paul I'd forgotten all about the money.

"Where'd they find it?"

"The robbers had it in that ghost town where you caught them."

I got a cigarette lit. It tasted a lot better than I expected.

"You shouldn't smoke."

"Yeah, I probably shouldn't."

She laughed. "I can see you're taking my medical advice to heart."

I said, genuinely curious, "Why'd you ever become a doctor, anyway?"

"My father was a doctor. And his father. My folks had only one child, me. They would've preferred a boy but I had to do."

"So they decided you should be a doctor, huh?"

She wore another Gibson girl outfit, the long print skirt, the high collar, the burnished bronze hair piled prettily on her long, narrow, pretty face. "Oh, no. They thought I should settle down and 'be sensible.' They even had my husband picked out. He was a doctor, of course. I'd be his wife. He had social ambitions. We'd move to Boston and he'd dazzle all of the upper crust. And I'd be the perfect wife. When I enrolled in medical school, my father did everything he could to get the dean to expel me.

"The dean wrote him a letter—I snuck into my father's office one night and read it—and said that he and all the male medical students had no choice but to accept me. It was the law. But then he said they'd harass me and drive me out, the way they had three previous female students. And they worked hard at it. They stained my clothes by spitting tobacco juice on me and they shouted every filthy name they could think of at me. Two of them nearly raped me in a dark basement one night until I pulled a small gun on them. And the dean himself planted a pint of whiskey in my room and tried to claim it was mine. He thought he was pretty smart until I got a lawyer who challenged him.

"Meanwhile, my father decided that if I could put up with all this, I must really want to be a doctor after all. So he told the dean to call off his dogs. The problem was, it was too late. They'd been set in motion. They didn't leave me alone the whole time I was there. But I do have to give my professors credit. They didn't like me or my sex much but they graded me fairly. I suppose they were afraid I might challenge them legally. I graduated at the top of my class."

"That's a hell of a story."

"Not if you'd had to live through it. There were times I really feared for my life. A female medical student in Kentucky had her throat cut one night by two surgery candidates. Some of the boys really get carried away."

She was putting her bottles of medicine back in her black bag. She said, "I put some magazines on the chair over there. They're old ones from my office. But I thought you might like them."

"I appreciate that."

She was being friendly, extending herself in a way she never had before. Maybe it was as simple as me being sick and her being a doctor. And yet there was a reserve in the way she spoke to me. She seemed so much freer with other people.

I said, and the words surprised me as much as they probably did her, "You don't like me much, do you?"

She glanced up after she finished closing her bag. "No, I guess I don't."

"Why not?"

She shook her head. "I've got things to do, Mr. Lamont. I don't have time to talk. I'm sorry."

"C'mon, now. Tell me."

She sighed. "You didn't do a very good job with your brother."

What could I say? "I know I didn't."

"He looked up to you. He did everything you asked of him."

"I didn't have anything to do with that robbery."

Her tone softened. "I know you didn't. And I also know I'm not being very nice. It's just—"

"It's just what?"

"You sent him out here on one of your 'errands.' If he hadn't come, he'd still be alive today."

I jammed out my cigarette and lit another one.

"Do you really need that?"

"Yeah," I said. "I do."

"You're angry."

"Yeah, I guess I am. You're blaming me for my brother's death."

She looked at me directly. "If you didn't feel some guilt about it, you wouldn't be so angry."

I took a deep drag, let the smoke out. It was blue in the dust-moted stream of sunlight.

I said, "I thought you told me that you were glad you had your time with him, even if it was short."

"I was being selfish, Mr. Lamont."

"Will you please quit calling me Mr. Lamont, dammit? My name's Bryce."

She picked up her bag. "I was being selfish, Bryce. It's Paul's life that mattered, not my feelings. I wish he'd never come out here. He'd still be alive. He could settle down with somebody else and have the family he'd always wanted. He was trying to make up for what you two boys didn't have after your folks died. Having a family was very important to him."

I was getting angry again. Not at her. At myself. At the bank robbers who'd come all the way from Canada.

I said, "How'm I doing with the malaria?"

"Coming along very well. Much better than I would have expected, given all you've been up to."

Now that we'd changed the subject, we both sounded relieved.

"You still getting lots of bodies?"

She shook her head. "Looks like the worst is over. At least for now. The cases we're seeing are more like yours. Debilitating but not fatal. The worst of them came from the swampland to the east. That's where the mosquitoes were the worst."

I smiled. "You like my nightshirt?"

"It's quite handsome."

"Is that a medical opinion?"

"No. My medical opinions you seem to disregard. That was a fashion opinion."

"I feel like I'm sixty in this thing."

"You should say a prayer that you *live* to be sixty. Night-shirt or not." She turned and walked to the door. "I'll check on you in a couple of days. Meanwhile, you should be able to be reasonably active for short periods of time."

I thought about standing up. But I was afraid I'd be wobbly. I didn't want to look any weaker or more feeble than I already felt.

"You could have dinner with me tonight or tomorrow night."

Quick, sad, half-embarrassed smile. "I really don't think that would be a very good idea for either of us, Bryce."

"Well," I said. "At least you called me Bryce."

"Yes," she said. "Yes, I did, didn't I?"

Then she was gone.

I had a couple of good hours there. Ate a good lunch of chili and wheat bread, drank a cool beer, had two or three delicious smokes, and then went for a twenty-minute walk in the sunshine.

I liked the town. It resembled an illustration in a magazine about living in the Midwest, from the friendly citizens to the spanking-clean streets kept that way by men in jail uniforms. Pekins had somehow convinced them to be polite. I imagined he had a few illegal but worthwhile methods to convince them.

I ended up, tired, on a park bench across from the county courthouse.

A couple of geezers were playing some kind of card game I didn't understand. They faced each other across a picnic table that the pigeons had bedecked with their splashing white favors from above. Every once in a while one of the geezers would yell out, "Damn right!" then slap down a card.

I dozed. I suppose some people thought I was drunk, a

man my age asleep on a park bench when the sunlight was so seductive and the day so merry.

Shouting woke me. At first I was disoriented.

I wondered if somebody had been shot. There was that much commotion, shouts, and cries.

A mob of people was collecting in front of the court-house doors.

"What's going on?" I said to one of the geezers.

He was irritated that I'd interrupted his game of Damn Right or whatever it was.

"Whyn't you go and find out fer yerself?"

" 'Cause I like to bother cranky old bastards like you."

His friend laughed. "You got that right, mister. He's about the crankiest sonofabitch in the whole valley."

The other one scowled. "The trial. Supposed to be a verdict any minute. Now is that enough for you?"

"Thank you. That's plenty."

"And don't you go callin' me cranky, either," he said to his friend. "You think *I'm* cranky. You should be around yourself when your rheumatism is actin' up. Then who's cranky?"

My nap had made me feel better. Amazing what fifteen minutes of sleep can do.

I got up and walked across the street. There were two reporters there with notebooks. There were also two men with cameras. Some of Pekins's men were clearing the court-house steps. They were being polite and gentle. Nobody got insulted or pushed around, but they were effective anyway. The steps were cleared.

Each person had a different way of waiting. A few stared at the sky. A few stared at their feet. A few whispered to friends. A few chewed tobacco. One man played a har-monica real nice and low.

"You remember our bet, I take it?" one merchant said to another.

"I wasn't that drunk. And I'll be happy to take your money."

"You got it t'other way around, Gil. They're gonna find her guilty."

"You sure don't know nothin' about this town of ours," the second merchant said. "He wronged her. She had every right to show him, according to most people in this town. He wronged her and he disgraced her and then he ran out on her. And she's spent most of her life alone. That kind of thing can unhinge a person, especially a sensitive woman like her. And that makes people feel sorry for her. That's why they're gonna find her not guilty."

"We'll see."

"You're damn right we'll see."

Right after that a cheer went up inside the courthouse. Her people cheering for her or the Wylie kin cheering for their dead kin?

The judge gaveled silence so loudly you could hear it way out here.

Finally, the silence came. He said something but from here you couldn't tell what it was.

And then the doors were bursting open and she was coming down the steps. She was a pretty woman, no doubt about that, and right now, surrounded by people trying to hug her, kiss her, or just touch her, she looked so relieved you couldn't help but be happy for her. She was crying and laughing at the same time, the way you sometimes do.

A carriage pulled up and she fought her way through the mob—Pekins's officers helping her, treating the citizens a little rougher this time, a new urgency in what they were doing— and then she was being taken away from us.

"I'll be a sonofabitch," said the merchant who'd lost the bet.

"You sure will be." His friend grinned.

I didn't remember it till an hour later when I was standing myself to a beer at the Fox Inn. The fever sometimes made me forget things that would only come back to me when I was feeling better.

They'd only found half the money, Laura had said. Then where was the other half? The thieves had stuck together. There was no reason to keep half with them and bury the other half, especially since they'd likely be going back to Canada again. So where would the other half be? Or was there another half at all?

I decided to stop in at the chief's office.

He was sitting on the edge of his desk smoking a pipe and talking to one of his deputies. His wife, or somebody, had made him a sling out of the same khaki material as his uniform. It looked pretty snappy.

The front was empty when I'd come in so I just walked back down the hall to where I heard voices.

Pekins stopped talking and said, "Help you with something, Lamont?" Not real happy to see me apparently.

"Like to talk to you."

"I'm pretty busy."

"I can wait out front till you're done."

He looked irritably at his deputy and rolled his eyes. He wanted to make real sure that I saw just how much he didn't want to talk to me.

"What is it you'd like to discuss?"

"That's kind of private."

"Samuels here can keep a secret."

"I'd still prefer to talk to you alone. No offense, Samuels."

Samuels just shrugged. "Hell, Chief, I'll go over to the courthouse and check on those land plats. Maybe get old Gus and Petra to quit pickin' at each other. I get real tired breakin' up their fistfights. It's almost obscene watchin' two eighty-three-year-olds beatin' the shit out of each other that way. I'll get the plat and settle this thing once and for all."

"Nice of you to leave me with Lamont here," Pekins said.

Samuels grinned, put on his campaign hat, then brushed past me into the hallway.

"You make a man feel right at home, Chief."

He didn't acknowledge what I said. He went around and sat behind his desk. He set his pipe down and said, "So when can I expect you to leave town?"

"Soon as I check out a few things."

"Such as."

"Such as why a gang of robbers would come all the way down from Canada to stick up a small bank here. I mean, unless I'm mistaken, Canada *does* have some pretty good–sized banks up there, correct? And also because I'm curious about why the robbers only had half the money on them when we got them. Who said it was half?"

"The bank said it was half."

"The bank being . . . ?"

"The bank being Mr. Jed Wylie."

"That's right. Mr. Jed Wylie. Who the hell'd know how much was in the vault except him?"

"The man who does the books."

"That'd be Grayson."

I thought of the nervous man with the boarder he didn't want, Stodla. I thought of his even more nervous, and very angry, wife.

"Grayson agrees that was half the money?"

"Grayson doesn't have to agree. Wylie is the boss and his word is good enough for me. Isn't it for you?"

"I don't know yet."

He picked up his pipe. Dragged on it. It was dead. He took a stick match from his khaki uniform shirt and ignited it on the edge of his thumbnail. He was nimble at it. He got his pipe going.

"What the hell are you trying to say, Lamont?"

"I don't know that, either."

Some more dragonlike puffing on his pipe.

"I'm sorry about your brother. He was a decent young man. I genuinely liked him. Laura brought him to a town picnic and *everybody* liked him. Not just me. But he's dead now and there's nothing we can do about it. The man who killed him is also dead. So at least there's been a small measure of justice. But it's done. The whole thing. Maybe we'll come across the other half of that money someday and maybe we won't. Moot point. Jed has insurance. They'll send out their own investigator and he'll try and stir up suspicion just the way you are and maybe in the end he'll find the other half of the money or maybe he won't. But either way the case will be closed once and for all." He eyed me coldly. "So I can't think of one good reason for you to stay in this town more than twenty-four hours more, can you?"

"You're running me out?"

"I'm gently suggesting you leave."

"And if I don't?"

"And if you don't I'll make you as miserable as I can. I'll enforce every law on the book. I'll be such a pest and such a nuisance you'll *want* to leave."

"You sound like you've had some practice at this."

"I have, believe me."

A knock. Another uniformed man. "The county attorney

wonders if you can run over there and sign some papers on the auction you held last weekend."

"My pleasure. Mr. Lamont was just leaving."

He got up. Came around the desk. Slight, trim, intelligent, efficient. Much more dangerous a foe than some beery bully.

"You remember what I said, Lamont."

"I'm pretty sure I will."

He smiled. "Train depot's not far. You could stop by and get your ticket in advance. That way you'd be sure not to miss your train."

"I appreciate the tip."

"My pleasure, Lamont. My pleasure."

THIRTEEN

I WENT HOME and slept for a few hours.

I dreamed about Paul again. But this time it wasn't a pleasant memory. It was the time he'd visited me in prison.

He looked young and scared. Some of the prisoners smirked at him. Even a couple of the guards nudged each other as he approached the table where I sat.

I wished that he hadn't come. I'd told him in many letters to just stay home and go on with his life and someday I'd get out and then I'd change my ways and we could all be happy again.

It was my twenty-fifth birthday was the thing. He just couldn't see me being alone on what to him was such an important day.

So he came up and spent an hour talking to me. He never did loosen up. Being in a prison intimidated him. The high walls. The armed guards. The scurvy prisoners. The air of barely contained rage, of perversion.

My kid brother. And in the dream, I tried to warn him.

Get away from me as fast and far as you can, kid. I know I'm your older brother and I know you look up to me and admire me but I'm a bum, kid. And I'll probably never change. I won't go back to bank robbing. But I'll always run a con on people. It's the only thing I know. And it's the only thing I like. There's nobody to blame for it. It's just the way I am. They want to "rehabilitate" me, that's the word some of the judges use these days. But how can you rehabilitate somebody who enjoys what he does?

I'd said that to the kid so many times, so many ways. To get away and stay away. Uncle Jim said it, too, that I wasn't any good, that I'd just get him in trouble.

The kid stayed fresh and clean. He never even dabbled in con games, though with that innocent face he could have become a prime predator.

Get away and stay away.

But he hadn't.

He'd been waiting at the prison gates for me. He'd brought a battered old wagon. He took me to town, where we laid over for quite a while. And I told him how I wanted to settle things with Jed. He said he'd go ahead a month or so and scope out things for me. Get the lay of the land, as it were. Meanwhile, I was to take a month and just enjoy myself. Do nothing but get used to the outside world again. He even had money for me. He insisted I take it, said he'd been working at a granary and had saved his money.

The rest, you know about.

The first thing I did when I woke up was throw up. I drank some water and went back to bed.

It was night when I came back. There'd been dreams but I didn't remember any of them.

Food began to appeal to me. A good meal. And then an evening stroll.

I got washed up and changed and went out into the night.

The lamps were lit. You could hear five different player pianos going at once, one from each saloon. The streets were empty of respectable people. They'd left the business area to the nighthawks and riffraff.

People down here now swaggered, staggered, stumbled. Some were working on a drunk, some had gone way beyond such a state already. They were just feeding a perpetual drunk they'd been on since before South Carolina had seceded from the Union.

I watched the night people from my window in the restaurant. They were my own kind. I was getting old enough, and honest enough, to admit that to myself now. A woman like Laura Westcott wasn't ever going to give me a chance because she knew better than I did what I was. Who could blame her?

I had a beer in the restaurant while I waited for my meal.

The woman was just bringing me my food when the front door opened and the Graysons came in. I almost didn't recognize them. Not only were they both dressed up in Sunday morning best—a dapper blue Edwardian-cut suit for the mister, a dark blue organdy dress with lots of ruffles for the missus—they were also smiling. No more dour faces. The smiles were a bigger surprise than the duds.

They had to walk past me to get to the lone empty table. When they got even with me, I looked up and said, "How's Mr. Stodla?"

At first, neither of them seemed to recognize me. They glanced at each other and then she said, "Oh, you're the man who came over last week."

"Yes."

"And asked about Stodla."

"Yes."

"He's gone."

This was the second time they'd surprised me.

"Gone? Where?"

"A hotel," Mr. Grayson said.

There was something troubling, suspicious about this—but I wasn't sure what.

"Were you expecting it?"

"Nosy cuss, aren't you?" Mr. Grayson said.

I half-expected the prim-looking Mrs. Grayson to say, Now that's not a very polite way to talk. Instead, she said to her husband, "That's just how he was with me the day he came over and asked all those questions."

"Enjoy your meal, Lamont," Grayson said, then let his wife lead him to the back of the restaurant.

I couldn't really relax and enjoy my meal. I was too aware of the Graysons sitting in the back. I was also too aware of something taking shape in front of me. It was like a form in the darkness. You know it's there but you can't quite make it out.

Pekins was satisfied that everything was fine. He was a good lawman. Smart and, I suspected, honest. His instincts should be good enough for me.

But maybe because Paul was my brother—and because I'd come to like both Krohn and Carmody—there was something about the whole bank robbery that bothered me.

What could I do? The thieves were dead and, according to the law, the case was closed.

Then why were the grim Graysons so happy and why had Stodla all of a sudden moved out? Hell, why had he moved *in* in the first place, when the Graysons so obviously didn't want him?

There was only one person who could answer that question and I decided to go looking for him.

I found Stodla down near the small dam, fishing. We used to do that a lot together, when we were between running cons and living on the profits.

Nothing fancy. He'd grown up in Kentucky where worms were considered to be the only thing a fishing man needed besides a pole. Forget all the other fancy theories.

He looked peaceful. He wore a pair of big faded overalls and a red shirt that could make you blind if you stared at it long enough. And no socks or shoes. If you stopped there, and didn't look at the cigarette he had set on a rock next to his pint of whiskey, you'd swear he was an overgrown prairie kid, all innocence.

"Hey, Lamont."

"Hey yourself."

"Where's your pole?"

"Didn't bring one on this trip."

"Sit down."

"No admission?"

"Not only no admission. Best seat in the house." He patted the ground next to him.

I sat. He wasn't kidding about the best seat in the house. Below the dam like this you got a nice sudsy view of the river and a good peek at the birch-lined island on the other side. Easy to imagine the Indian days, a line of birch-bark canoes along the far shore, glimpses of braves flashing between the trees, drums pounding messages back and forth, little Indian children playing on the grassy spot several hundred yards to the west. That was all gone. The Army and illness and bad luck and hotheads on both sides had seen to it that the majority of Indians were transferred to camps and reservations. White men used the island for hunting now. I'm told it was a pheasant hunter's dream come true in late October, early November.

"Sorry about your brother."

"Thanks."

"I only met him that one time, but he sure struck me as a nice kid."

"He was."

"And seein' him with that lady doctor, they sure looked good together."

"Yeah. They did."

"I figured they'd have kids and all. Everybody did. Not a man around could get to her until that brother of yours showed up. Then she was just as giggly as any other girl." He'd been watching his line as he talked. Now he looked at me. "Am I talking too much about your brother?"

"It's all right. I'm glad you liked him."

We both watched the water for a time. Downstream you could see some other fishermen in a rowboat. It was kind of funny, and it sort of came to me as a revelation, sitting there with Stodla and realizing suddenly that he'd changed a lot. There was still all the menace and bluster but these days you could see past it and see that most of it was an act. There was a sorrow and a fear in him now, the sorrow and fear of a scared boy, something you didn't expect in a man as violent as Stodla. I knew better than to say any of this to him. Because then his pride would be hurt and he'd take great pleasure in giving me a bloody nose and a smashed lip.

"This is a good place to live," he said.

Which surprised me. "You thinking of settling down?"

"Sure. Hell, I've had my day. Drinkin' and whorin' and scammin'. I'm almost forty now. I got me the gout, the rheumatiz, the hemorrhoids, my left eye's goin' bad on me, and I got this ringin' in my ears sometimes. And I can't get the same kind of hard-on I used to when I was younger. I can still get it up with no trouble but it won't stand up and salute the way it used to. You know what I mean?"

"Hell," I said, "sounds like I should just take you out and shoot you."

He laughed. "Yeah, just like an old dawg who's run his course."

"What'll you do for a living?"

He pinched his mouth as if he was going to scold me. "I almost don't want to tell ya. Way you always talk about Jed and all." He went back to fishing.

"So what's Jed gonna do for you?"

"Just don't run him down, all right?"

"All right."

"Promise?"

"Promise."

" 'Cause he's just been so damned nice to me my whole life, Bryce, even if you couldn't see it."

"So what's he gonna do for you?" I said.

"Horse ranch. He's buying this big stud farm over to the north and he's gonna have me take care of it for him." He fixed me with a steely gaze. "Now, you don't say nothin' nasty about him."

"That's great. It really is."

Then after a time, I said, "Bet you're glad to be out of Grayson's, huh?"

He shook his head. "Boy, they were somethin'. 'Bout the crabbiest people I ever met."

"Why'd you stay there, anyway?"

He shrugged. "No big deal. They were havin' some kind of audit at the bank—you know, after Jed's brother got killed and all—and Jed wasn't sure he could trust Grayson or not. Thought he might be embezzling or something and might try to get out of town. So he convinced Grayson to let me stay at his house for a month while the audit was done. That way, I could keep a close eye on Grayson."

"Spy on him, I guess, huh?"

He made another sour face. "See? There you go. Sure, I was spyin' on him, like you say. But didn't Jed have that right? After all, with his brother dead, it was his bank now."

I'd never heard it put that simply before, that directly. With his brother out of the way, Jed had clear title to the bank where he'd been just number two for several years.

"Anyways," he said, "Jed paid ya off and he didn't have to. He coulda stalled. Or he coulda just had ya run out of town. You know that, don't ya?"

"Yeah, I guess I do."

"He likes ya. And he's sorry you had to spend that time in prison. And so he figured that he'd help ya out by just payin' up and handin' ya the money. He did a little time in jail, too, them years ya didn't see him."

"Jed? In jail?"

"Yeah. My mother was ailin' so I had to head back to Kansas. Jed went on up to Canada. There was this gal. You know how Jed is with gals. There was this gal and he followed her all the way up into Canada. She was married but he didn't give a shit. Ya ask me, I think he likes 'em married. Makes it more excitin' for him."

Stodla pulled his pole out of the water and checked the hook. The worm was still on there. He threw the line back in. "Anyways, he followed her all the way there without realizin' that her old man is a judge. Can you fuckin' believe that? A judge? Not that that slows him down any. He kept seein' this woman on the sly and started runnin' a couple of scams up there. Real little ones. Just sorta to keep his hand in and buy him bourbon money. Nothin' serious. But this one time—and you talk about bad luck—he's scammin' this fella in a bar and the fella turns out to be a deputy lawman or whatever they call 'em up there. He arrests Jed on the spot. And next mornin', Jed's in court. And I don't have to tell ya who the judge is, do I? And o' course the judge, he knows who Jed is. He's the fella destroyin' his life and tryin' to steal his wife. So he gives him six months in jest about the dirtiest, vilest jail you ever heard of. Jed lost fifty pounds in there and developed a couple rashes he still can't get rid of."

Stodla faced me. "So what I'm sayin' here, Bryce, is the reason he gave you that money so fast and all is he's got a pretty good idea of what you went through when you were in prison. And he's sorry we had to run out on you that time. And he also wants you to know how sorry he is about your brother. He lost a brother, too, remember."

"Yeah, I know he did."

"I know you won't ever like him or trust him, Bryce. But you got to admit, every once in a while, he does somethin' real nice for folks, including me and you."

"Yeah, I guess he does at that." I stood up and stretched.

"Hey, where you goin'?"

"Back to town. I need to get some more medicine. Lay it in for the next bout."

"Seems like you're over the worst of it."

"Yeah, I am. But every forty-eight, seventy-two hours, it's gonna be back."

"How long's that last?"

"Couple weeks, maybe my whole life. They just don't know yet."

"Well, that lady doc's plenty smart. If anybody can help ya, she can."

I leaned down and patted his bearlike shoulder. "You're a good man, Stodla."

"I just wish you felt that way about Jed."

"Maybe I will someday, maybe I will."

All the way back to town I thought about Jed's time in jail, up there in Canada. Jail would be a real likely place to meet a gang of bank robbers.

They were having a funeral in the Methodist church. I recognized a couple of the nurses from the hospital. Likely this was another malaria case.

I stopped in at the police station but Pekins was gone. I headed on over to the library.

Three local families were prominent enough to have small sections about them, their original origins, when they'd come to this area, and how they'd managed to become prominent.

I had no idea what I was looking for, just something about Jed Wylie and his kin that would suggest something intriguing to me. There was nothing.

Only one article stopped me. The one about Jed's brother Donald getting engaged to Jenny Rice.

A gang comes down from Canada. That was one unlikely story. An otherwise reputable spinster shoots and kills her upstanding fiancé for cheating on her. That's another unlikely story. And who was the *femme fatale* involved, the one who took Donald away? Her name was listed in only one of the articles about Jenny Rice's address, a "Miss Susan Baxter of Daly City."

If I recalled correctly, Daly City was only about two hours away by train. I stopped by the pharmacy and bought some more quinine. Laura Westcott was sitting at one of the little ice cream tables in the back, having coffee.

I got myself a cup and joined her.

"How're you feeling?" she asked.

"Pretty good, actually."

"Just remember the forty-eight/seventy-two-hour swing. It'll get bad for you in there somewhere. Four, five hours of fevers and chills and then you'll be all right again for the next couple of days."

"I've never heard of a disease like this one."

"Been with us a long time," she said. "There was an article in a medical journal about how the Aztecs tried to combat it."

"They have much luck?"

"Not so's you'd notice." She looked tired. "Two more dead."

"I saw the funeral."

"That was a couple of days back. Two more dead just last night. Though it finally seems to be tapering off. The temperature is dropping steadily every day. That should help with that swampy area up near Grinder's Pass."

"That's where most of them are coming from?"

"As far as we can tell." Then, "How about you? What're you up to?"

I told her about this Miss Susan Baxter. "Anybody ever see her?" I asked.

She shook her head. "I wouldn't know. I was too busy—" She hesitated. "Falling in love with your brother."

I went right past that one. I didn't know what to say. She had her grief and I had mine and I still had feelings for her and I felt like a total shit about having them. But there you were.

"Funny she didn't testify at the trial," I said.

"I suppose it is," she said, "now that you mention it." She stood up. "I'm glad you're feeling better, Bryce."

"Thanks to you, I am."

She waved my compliment away. "I just wish that was true. If it was, it would mean I could help the others, too.

I've got a six-year-old boy in the hospital and I don't think he's going to make it." Her eyes glistened. "I was thinking he looked a little like your brother. Same kind of nose and chin. You know, boyish. If Paul and I'd had a child, he'd probably have looked just like him."

"That's nice to think about."

She snuffled up her tears. "I'm setting a real good example for the town, standing here blubbering."

"More people should blubber, and more often. Blubbering is good for the soul."

She smiled. "Actually, it is. And you're right. More people *should* blubber."

For the second time, she touched me. Put her hand gently on my shoulder. Not for long, but I got chills. And this time it wasn't malaria.

"It was nice to see you, Bryce. Good luck with Susan Baxter."

"I'll let you know how I come out."

The train trip was pleasant. Before leaving the pharmacy, I'd bought a magazine of detective stories and a couple good cigars. Now I read, I smoked, I dozed.

Wisconsin seemed to be beautiful no matter where you looked. We passed a lot of small lakes, a lot of limestone hills, a lot of deep hardwood forest. Deer stood watching us pass. Farmers waved. A kid on a calico raced us till his mount just gave out.

I noticed that the temperature kept declining, too. Nothing dramatic but it was heading downward. That's one thing about a Midwestern summer. They tend to boil for three months straight—except in the middle, when there's always a kind of autumnal rehearsal. Just checking on autumn to see if it's all ready to go when the time comes. It'll run in the low sixties and high fifties for six, seven days. You won't be able to sleep with the windows open during this time and the baseball players will freeze their asses off if the games go into early twilight.

I hoped for everybody's sake that we were coming into this period. Goodbye, mosquitoes.

Daly City had about five thousand citizens. It was a small rail hub that mostly serviced farmers in the surrounding area. It had been passed over as county seat ten years ago and folks hereabouts were still bitter about it. An old man on the train told me all this.

There was a fancy new two-story brick bank on one corner. Actually, the bank was downstairs, and the local government upstairs. I went upstairs.

I told the clerk that I was a Pinkerton man looking for a woman who had come into some money. She didn't know it yet and we'd had a difficult time finding her. I showed her my fake Pinkerton business card. There was a former Pinkerton man who ran a print shop in Omaha and he was real good at trumping up identification cards. He wasn't cheap but he was sure as hell reliable.

The clerk had trouble finding a Susan Baxter, too. An office like this, there are several ways they can cross-check a name. One set of books or another was bound to have some reference to her if she'd lived here for any amount of time. She'd paid taxes or she'd paid a fine or she'd applied for a license or she'd bought a house, something anyway that would show up in the city office.

"Gosh, she must sure keep to herself," the skinny lady with the fat hairy mole told me. "We have just one notation about her. She opened a dress shop and applied for a retail license."

"Is the dress shop still in business?"

"Far as I can tell. It's not one I've ever been to. Too fancy for my tastes."

She wrote down the address for me.

I thanked her.

"She coming into a *lot* of money, is she?"

"Not a lot," I said. "Just enough to buy a palace or two."

The woman flushed. She was a good gal. "Gosh, can you imagine somebody knocking on your door and telling you you've got all that money?"

Before I visited the dress shop, I stopped in a saloon and had a beer and a couple of hard-boiled eggs.

I still wasn't sure how I was going to approach her. I wasn't going to use the inheritance story or the Pinkerton tale. Too easy to check.

I had a second beer but it didn't make me any smarter. I was still nervous about approaching her. There was something here, I was sure of that, but I didn't want to scare it away.

M'Lady's Fashions was housed in a one-story stucco business building that was split right down the center. The other half of the building was Sam Watkins—Saddles.

A bell tinkled overhead as I stepped inside and a dozen perfumes rushed to not merely seduce but pulverize me.

I didn't see anybody.

There were several mannequins showing off what the demure signs claimed were "the latest fashions from Paris, New York, and Chicago." They all looked pretty much the same. They had bustles, corsets, and low-cut necks. As we approached the century mark, the sophisticated ladies were showing off more of themselves and demanding to smoke cigarettes in public and vote. All of which was fine with me.

Blouses, belts, hose, shoes, undergarments, the store seemed to have just about anything m'lady could ask for.

And then a voice said, "I'll be damned." The voice was familiar but I couldn't put a face to it until I turned around.

She was ten years older than the last time I'd seen her but she'd lost none of her buxom, redheaded impact. She was one of those thirtyish women who could be a convincing whore or society lady. Here, she wore a tailored suit that hid her ample gifts. Or tried, anyway. Nothing, not even a loose sack, could hide a body as rich as hers.

"Susan Baxter," I said.

She laughed. "You like it?"

"Good as any other name, I guess."

"I did a little time down Waco way. Decided I should change my handle when I got out."

"What was it the last time I saw you?"

"Adriana Falworth."

"Ah, yes, you were a duchess. How'd you end up out here?"

"Have some kin not far from here. Decided it was time to settle down."

I looked around. "How's this going?"

"Not as well as I'd hoped. But it's doing all right. I can pay my bills, anyway." She watched me with those soft, smart brown eyes of hers. She watched me carefully and listened to me carefully. She sensed I was here for no good purpose. Every few moments I'd see her lower lip tremble almost imperceptibly. She was putting on a good show but that's all it was—a show.

"You see much of Jed?" I asked.

"Jed? No. His brother Donald? Yes. We were going to get married, in fact."

"I hear they were very different kinds of people."

She forced a smile. "That's why I took up with him. If he'd been anything like Jed . . ."

"I guess he had a nice woman, his fiancée. Donald, I mean."

She started straightening some of the merchandise: blouses, ribbons, belts. "Yes, he said she was very nice. He was very concerned about her, as a matter of fact. How she'd handle it when he told her about us."

"You weren't worried about his seizures?"

"His seizures?"

"You knew he was epileptic, right?"

"Oh, the epilepsy." She wasn't as good as she used to be. Maybe she hadn't stayed in practice. Maybe she'd gone straight for a while and come back to it. Everything she'd said about Donald was hollow. "Well, he seemed to have it pretty much under control."

I'd made up the epilepsy part and she'd walked right into it. "So you had big wedding plans and all?"

"That's what he wanted, a big wedding."

"This sure is a nice shop." We were into a certain rhythm and I wanted to break it. Wanted her to be wary of what I'd say next. So I changed the subject abruptly, hoping to keep her off balance.

"Thanks. Its my pride and joy, actually."

"In fact, I'd like to buy something."

"You would?"

"Yes, a blouse. You know, the kind that go with those Gibson girl outfits."

"I love those."

I described Laura Westcott.

"She sounds pretty. She somebody special?"

"Very."

She smiled. "Kinda funny, isn't it? All the things we used to do and now I wind up here in Podunkville, running a dress shop, and you're inclined to a respectable woman."

"Yeah, it is kinda funny. Both of us going straight about the same time."

Her lower lip was trembling again. A vague panic began to show in her intelligent brown eyes. "Well, you wanted to see blouses, didn't you?"

"Yes, I did."

So we looked at blouses. I decided, what the hell, to make this serious. I picked out a blouse I figured would go good with those outfits Laura Westcott wore.

"You got any fancy wrapping?" I asked.

"Sure."

"And a big bow?"

"A real big one."

"Great. Wrap it up."

Maybe it was her nerves or maybe she just wasn't deft with gift wrapping. Her fingers were so shaky, she managed to wrinkle the paper in several places. The ribbon didn't lie right on the edges of the package. And the bow was all mooshed down by the time she got done affixing it.

Well," she said, "how do you like that?"

"It's beautiful. You're very good."

"I wrinkled it in a couple of places."

"She'll never notice."

She told me how much and I paid her and as she was handing me my change, I said, "You must've saved up quite a bit to buy this place."

The panic became more obvious in her eyes. A frantic smile. "Oh, let's just say I had some luck on a riverboat."

"A wealthy older gentleman, no doubt."

"My specialty."

"You were always the best. Did Donald want you to keep the shop after you were married?"

For just a moment there she looked like a kid taking a

test and not knowing the right answer. "Uh—yes, he did. He said why not? He said he knew how much I loved this place and I should keep it."

"He sure sounds like a nice man."

"He was."

I stared straight at her and said, "Funny they didn't ask you to testify at the trial."

"They did."

"They did?"

She nodded. "The local doctor here, he wrote them a letter and said that I just couldn't handle the pressure of testifying and that they should let me testify by letter."

I could imagine the sweet pressure she'd applied to the local doctor to write such a letter.

"He was the love of my life."

"Donald?"

"Yes."

"I guess Jed was broken up, too," I said.

"He loved Donald. He really did."

I took out my watch. "Well, time to head back. It's really been nice seeing you, Miss Baxter."

She smiled. "Sure never thought I'd run into you again, Bryce."

We shook hands the way men do.

The bell tinkled on my way out.

"If you see Jed, give him my best," she said.

"Sure," I said. "Sure, I'll be glad to."

I stayed in town another two hours, asked a lot of people a lot of questions. And got just about the answers I expected.

FOURTEEN

SUSAN BAXTER WAS a con dating back to our Kansas City days and one of Jed's old lovers. They'd had some troubled times, one of those relationships that teetered back and forth between rage and lust. She'd tried half-seriously to kill him a couple of times and he'd beaten her up on more than one occasion. As I remembered it, they'd pretty much fought to a draw.

She'd had good reason to be nervous when I was in her little shop.

I'd made up the bit about Donald's epilepsy, but she'd gone for it; and her story about not seeing much of Jed hadn't sounded true at all.

I also gave some thought to Stodla. Jed had forced him upon the Graysons for some reason that Stodla couldn't or didn't want to understand. Grayson figured in all this, but how? He looked too skittish to be a part of anything criminal.

Then there was Jed himself. If his brother hadn't died,

he'd still be a bank employee. But now, he ran the bank and de facto became the town's most powerful citizen. Just the kind of role Jed would enjoy playing.

And finally, there was one more person I needed to talk to: Jenny Rice herself. Only she could confirm the behavior of her fiancé during the months he was allegedly seeing Susan Baxter. I wasn't sure she'd see me but I had to try.

I looked at the gift box on my lap. Wondered what Laura would say. Wondered what I *wanted* her to say.

I fell asleep.

It was night when I got back to town. The temperature had dropped a few more degrees. It was time for a jacket or at least a heavier shirt.

The lights and noise from the saloons were helping the reddish dusk sky turn darker. A drunk tottered along the side of the main street followed by a yipping little dog looking for attention and affection. The drunk was too caught up in himself to notice.

I stopped by the hospital. The funeral home wagon was out front. They were busy inside. There were two benches in the lobby filled with people in various stages of fever. None of them looked too bad, just groggy.

The staff was frantic. They moved faster than I'd ever seen them move. A couple of nurses smiled at me and hurried on. They glanced curiously at the gift box I had in my hand.

I found her on the second floor. She was ministering to a two-year-old in a small white bed. The child was crying, scared. Laura picked her up, rocked her, and hummed some ancient Scottish song of the sea. She even sang a few lines in the ancient tongue. The child was calmed.

I watched all this, feeling as if I were a Peeping Tom.

For one thing, this wasn't a scene familiar to my cynical eyes. For another, I wanted her. It wasn't just lust, either. It was more than that and it was frightening for that reason. I'd never wanted more than sex after Marsha left me.

After the child was asleep, Laura put her back in her bed and then hurried down the row of children's beds, checking on each kid. Most of them slept. Malaria had to be particularly hard on the little ones and the very old ones.

When she was done, she turned back toward the doorway where I stood. She waved and came forward.

She took my elbow and guided me to a small office down the hall. I wanted her to keep her hand on me. At the moment, it felt more intimate than a kiss.

The office was a dumping ground for medical books and journals, piled everywhere.

"As you can see, we're very proud of our shared office here," she said. "We're usually more orderly than this but with all the malaria . . ." She shrugged and sat on one side of the desk. I sat on the other.

I pushed the gift box to her.

"Oh, gosh."

"Go ahead. I thought you might need a little pick-me-up."

Her lovely face became grim. "I had a bad spell this afternoon. For lunch, I walked up to the cemetery. Bad mistake. I came apart. I wasn't good for anything for two hours. And they really need my full concentration here."

I just wanted her to open it.

I just wanted to see her happy.

"Go ahead," I said.

"I don't know if this is right, Bryce."

"Just open it. I think you'll like it."

She started slowly, reluctantly, tearing the edge of the

gift wrapping carefully, as if she might want to put it back in place and didn't want to damage it any more than necessary. She picked up speed as she went. "It's beautiful wrapping."

"Yeah, it's very nice."

"And really a beautiful bow."

"Keep going," I said.

Then, just before she got it open, she said, "I've been thinking, Bryce." She seemed nervous.

I smiled. "Just open it. We'll talk later."

She made a face I couldn't read exactly and proceeded to finish opening the box. She brought out the blouse and held it up and said, "It's so delicate."

"Like you."

She flushed. "I'm hardly delicate, Bryce. I don't even *want* to be delicate. I'm a doctor. I need to be strong. Delicate isn't something I especially admire."

"I just wanted you to know that even though my brother is gone—I'm here. Anytime you want to talk or just be with somebody who understands—"

She made that face again, the one I couldn't read. "Bryce," she said, "I can't accept this."

"Are you kidding?"

"No. No, I'm not."

"But why? Aren't we friends?"

She hesitated. "No, no, we're not friends, Bryce. I don't even know you."

"I'm Paul's brother."

"You two are nothing alike. Nothing. There isn't even a real family resemblance."

I laughed. "Yeah, the kid always said one of us was adopted."

She folded the blouse neatly and put it back in its box.

"This was awfully nice of you." She put the lid on the box and the box on the desk and pushed it back to me. "But I can't accept it."

"The kid would want you to have it."

"No, he wouldn't." She averted her eyes, sighed deeply, looked back at me. "You know what he was afraid of, Bryce?"

"What?"

"That you'd steal me from him."

"Oh, bushwah."

"No, really. He talked about that several times, about how you were so successful with women. He was afraid you'd come to town and seduce me and take me away from him. It was a real fear of his. He said you'd done that to several friends of yours, taken their women away like that."

I shrugged. "I did a lot of things I'm ashamed of, Laura. But I've changed. I really have."

"But don't you see that's what you're doing now?"

"I'm not following you."

"You're trying to steal me away from him."

"He isn't even alive."

"No," she said, "not physically, he isn't. But emotionally and spiritually, he is. He's very alive in my mind. And you're trying to steal me away from his memory. He's only been dead a few days, Bryce, and already you're bringing me presents. Can't you see what you're doing?"

"I just saw the blouse and figured you'd like it. Nothing more sinister than that."

"Well, I do like it."

"Then keep it."

She sounded irritated now. "Did you hear anything I just said to you?"

"Of course."

"Then you know why I can't keep it."

I sighed. "You really want me to take it back?"

"Yes. Or give it to somebody else." Then, "I need to get back to work, Bryce."

She stood up. Came around the desk. Picked up the box from the desk. Set it in my hands.

"Maybe it's time for you to leave town, Bryce. I don't want this situation to get out of hand."

"Don't worry. I won't bother you anymore."

She put a hand on my shoulder, the way a big sister would. "I loved him, Bryce. It's going to take me a long time to even think about another man. A long, long time. And that man—he's going to have to be like Paul, not like you. Not all swagger and polish and bad intentions."

"I'm not like that."

She threw her head back and laughed. "Oh, Bryce, of *course* you're like that. It's probably in your blood. You don't know any other kind of life and you never will. You're not a killer, thank God. But you're amoral."

"That one I resent."

"You don't think it's true? We buried Paul less than two days ago and here you are with a gift already?"

"A gift of friendship."

She hesitated. "Bryce, if I said, Let's go to my sleeping room and spend the night together, you'd say fine. You wouldn't even *think* about Paul. Or let me correct that. I think there's just enough morality in your heart that you'd *think* about him for a few seconds. You'd say to yourself that what you were about to do was wrong—was really betraying his memory—but then you'd go ahead and do it anyway." Then, "Can you deny it?" She took her hand away from my shoulder. "I need to get back to work, Bryce."

• • •

I had two choices. Get drunk or do some work.

Luckily, I was able to combine them. I visited all five of the town's saloons and taverns and asked my questions at each.

I don't know that I was all that subtle but then, I wasn't dealing with subtle people. They knew who I was: Paul's brother. Those who'd known him liked him, and those who hadn't known him had heard he was a decent young man. So they didn't mind talking about him and his malaria and everything.

And then I'd work the conversation around to the trial. I talked about Paul writing me some letters about it, how he couldn't decide if Jenny Rice should be found guilty or not. And then I mentioned that it was too bad a nice lady like Jenny would wind up with a man like Donald Wylie.

And nearly all the answers were the same: That was the funny thing about Don Wylie. He was just as nice as Jenny. He was just about the last person you'd expect to throw her over that way. And I said, well, that Susan Baxter must really be something. Maybe she was just so good-looking he couldn't help himself. And they said they wouldn't know—they'd never seen her.

Which was the same response I'd gotten in Daly City. Seems like nobody had ever actually seen them together. Heard plenty about it during the trial, how they'd trysted and how she was so seductive and all, and how Donald had pushed poor Jenny Rice away with no consideration whatsoever for her feelings.

But actually see this here Susan Baxter and Donald Wylie together?

Not actually.

Curious; damned curious.

•   •   •

The lights were on so I knocked.

Mrs. Grayson opened the door and said, "What're you doing here?"

"Just wanted to see your husband."

"He's asleep."

"Who is it?" a male voice said from the back of the house.

"He must be talking in his sleep," I said.

"He doesn't want to talk to you."

He came in from what was apparently the kitchen, holding a small glass of beer. He wore a faded shirt and loose, wrinkled trousers. He was only a dapper banker during the day.

"I need to talk to you, Mr. Grayson."

"About what?"

Mrs. Grayson crossed her arms. "I already told him you didn't want to talk to him."

"About the bank robbery."

They did me the favor of looking at each other nervously as soon as I mentioned the robbery.

"You talk to Mr. Wylie about that," she said.

"Or Chief Pekins," he said.

"He doesn't know anything about that robbery," she said.

"Not a darned thing," he said.

"So you go on now and get about your business," she said.

"It's past our bedtime already," he said.

"We're tired, too, folks our age," she said.

It was jabber, but filled with anxiety.

I said, "Did you like Donald Wylie?"

"He was a gentleman and a decent man," she said.

"He treated everybody very, very well," he said.

"Including you?"

"Especially him," she said.

"I had a stroke last year," he said.

"And Donald kept him on full pay all four months he was down," she said. "God bless him."

"You like his brother Jed?"

Another one of those anxious glances at each other.

"He has a different style from his brother," he said cautiously.

"Meaning you don't like him?"

"Don't put words in his mouth," she said.

"I didn't say I didn't like him," he said.

"He just said he has a different style is all," she said.

But I had my answer.

"Now if you don't mind," she said.

"I'm dead on my feet," he said.

"You shouldn't go calling on decent people this time of night anyway," she said.

"You think there's any chance that Jed was behind his own bank robbery?" I said.

They looked shocked, shocked that I'd figured it out, but not surprised. They didn't look surprised at all. Because they'd known for a long time what had been going on.

"You keep the bank's books," I said. "You've known what was going on there, didn't you? Was Jed dipping into the vault and Donald found out? Is that what forced him to rob his own bank? To cover up what he embezzled before the auditors came? If he had a robbery, nobody'd ever know any money was missing, now would they? And insurance would just cover it fine."

The last few sentences, Mrs. Grayson was busy pushing me back through the door into the night.

"So where's the money now, Mr. Grayson?" I asked through the still open door.

That was when Mrs. Grayson slammed the door so hard the entire house shook.

I went down the street, drank a few more beers and played a little pool, and then went up to my hotel room. It had been a long day and I didn't have any trouble sleeping.

He was pretty quiet for a man his size. He came in, pulled a chair up to my bed, and got the lamp lit before I even stirred. When I woke up, he was holding a pint of good blended whiskey in one hand and a .45 in the other. Shadows frolicked on the walls from the kerosene lamp; the bed smelled of sleep warmth.

"Mrs. Grayson wouldn't approve," I said. "She doesn't like men who call on decent people late at night."

"Well," Jed said, "then I guess we're even up because I don't approve of Mrs. Grayson. Nosy little bitch. He should've killed her years ago."

I took his bottle, had a swig, handed it back. I sat up and tumbled a cigarette free from the box. The first couple of drags tasted so fucking fine.

He said, "So you went and figured it out, huh?"

"Yeah. Grayson told you, huh?"

"Uh-huh. Came barreling out to my house, pounding on the door. Said you'd figured everything out." He took a swig. "You going to be reasonable about this?"

"Meaning what?"

"Meaning you can't prove jack shit. But I'm going to pay you off anyway."

"My brother's dead."

"I didn't kill him."

"In a way, you did."

"Goddamnit, Bryce, I told those stupid pricks not to hurt anybody. You know me. I'm not a killer."

Actually, I believed him. I was sure he'd told the gang

not to hurt anybody. And true enough, he wasn't a killer. He was a con like the rest of us and violent cons don't last long.

I took another drag. Six, seven drags they lose their taste. You're just feeding your habit.

"That why you had Stodla staying with the Graysons? So he could keep an eye on them until the robbery was over?"

He nodded, offered me the bottle. I shook my head.

"Grayson does the books. He found out I'd embezzled a lot. The only way I could make it right was to replace the money. But getting it from the family trust would be too suspicious. So I staged the robbery."

"I tracked you to Canada. You must've been in jail with the gang at one time."

"I was. They weren't any prizes, believe me. But I figured they could pull off a simple fucking robbery without hurting anybody. They'd done a lot of work along the Montana border back a couple of years earlier and nobody'd been killed."

"What if Grayson tells all this to Pekins?"

"He can't. I paid him off. If I go to prison, so does he. And I'm sure Mrs. Grayson wouldn't stand for that."

"I can't imagine Grayson taking a bribe."

"He has a cob up his ass, that's true. But he was also putting it to one of the gals who works in the back."

Grayson was?"

He grinned. "Wouldn't think he could even get it up, would you? Anyway, I found out about it and threatened to tell his old lady. Plus I gave him a grand."

"I still can't believe it."

"The other funny thing is, the one he's dicking?"

"Yeah?"

"She's a good-looking woman."

"*Gray*son?"

"Maybe he reads her Bible stories while they're humping or something." Then, "So how much do you want?"

"All of it."

The amiability was gone instantly and forever. I knew it would be. I wanted it to be. I would never be able to repay him in kind for the death of my brother—it was true, he was only marginally responsible—but I could sure make him suffer.

"Are you crazy, Bryce?"

"Nope. I want every penny that got taken from that bank."

"But why?"

"Doesn't matter why. All that matters is that I want it by six tomorrow night or I go to Pekins."

"And Pekins does what, exactly?"

"Starts an investigation. You've got yourself a bright boy in this little burg, Jed. He knows what he's doing."

"You're out of your fucking mind, Bryce, you know that?"

"I guess we'll see, won't we?"

"I don't believe this. I came up here wanting to be fair with you."

"You are being fair with me, Jed. You're going to give me all the money you took from your bank."

"That's not going to happen, Bryce." He did look truly amazed, and betrayed. He'd expected me to be reasonable on his terms. But with my brother dead, I didn't feel like being reasonable on anybody's terms but my own.

"I need some sleep, Jed."

"You bastard." He stood up. "I could shoot you right here and right now, you know that?"

"Yeah, I guess you could. But you'd have a hard time explaining why you shot an unarmed man in his own bed."

"You bastard."

"You're getting tired, too, Jed. Using the same cussword over again. Get yourself a little sleep and you'll think of a lot of new words. Now, please turn out the lamp."

"I'll turn out the fucking lamp, all right. Right on your fucking head is where I'll fucking turn it out, too."

"G'night, Jed."

"You bastard."

"See," I said, "you really do need some sleep."

He cursed me a few more times and left.

FIFTEEN

THE FEVER CAME right on schedule. Trains should run so well.

I had a couple of snorts of whiskey and sat in my long underwear on my bed, reading a dime novel. The damned things are so silly, and such bullshit, I don't know why I bother. Maybe I want to be Nick Carter when I grow up. A fella could do worse, I suppose.

An hour later, the chills came and I slogged down some quinine. Someday they'll probably figure out a way to make this stuff palatable. Maybe.

I got tired and then I got sick. The dime novel slipped from my fingers to the floor and I managed to push myself underneath the covers, which took about all the strength I had.

I slept.

I woke up a couple of times to use the thundermug but otherwise I stayed in bed for the next six hours. I had dreams and I had nightmares and I had a couple of pretty good erections, too—useless ones, needless to say.

And then it passed, the worst of it anyway.

I pissed a little and puked a little and then hauled my ass down the hall to revel in the big metal tub into which the dour maid poured hot water. I sipped whiskey while I sat there and soaked. I also tried to figure out what to do next.

I decided that since I had no impression of Jenny Rice at all—except for the one made when Jed slapped her in court, and that was far more about Jed than Jenny—I'd best pay a call on her.

But what pretext to use? We had no friends in common. We had no interests—that I knew of—in common. And we'd never met before.

Why would I come knocking on her door?

I went back down the hall and got dressed, feeling pretty good. The fever is always like a blackout. You feel brand new, and separate from it.

I went to the café and had roast beef and potatoes and gravy. I also had a cigar and two cups of scalding coffee.

I still hadn't come up with a good excuse to go see her. I was starting to get a headache from worrying the damned problem so much.

I didn't get my answer until late in the afternoon when I saw a nurse walk by in her starchy white uniform. I remembered how her attorney had extolled her public service during the trial. She'd helped with malaria cases at the hospital, before all this began.

I went to the livery stable and rented a horse for the day. I was still feeling wobbly. Then I hurried over to the general merchandise store. I didn't want to spend too much but I didn't want to spend too little. I had to make it look like

something unsophisticated men would come up with. A nice
black leather pair of gloves was what I ended up with.

I also bought a stamp and piece of paper and wrote out
the letter. I didn't make it too corny. Again, corny wasn't
something the men I'd seen at the hospital would write.
They'd be blunt and to the point.

I got everything fixed up and set off on my horse.

Dusk was settling in, the sky the color of fancy rouge,
the air cooler, stars already clear in the canopy of night.
This is always the most melancholy time of day for me and
I can never decide which quick fix I need most—a drink,
sex, or cutting my wrists.

Her house was a nice one, a mansion of sorts by local
standards, a two-story brick affair with a white veranda running the length of the front, and a central window on the
second floor set directly above the front door on the first
floor. The veranda had elaborate post brackets and a brack-
eted cornice. I knew a little something about architecture
because I'd run a couple of housing scams once upon a
time.

A Negro maid answered the door. She wasn't in uniform.
She wore a plain housedress. She was maybe forty with a
nice body.

"Yes, mister?"

"I'd like to see Miss Rice."

"I'm afraid she's in the gazebo."

"Couldn't I go out there and see her?"

She looked as if I'd just suggested something extremely
vulgar. "This is her lonesome time."

"Her lonesome time?"

"Yes sir, that's what she's always called it. When she
can be all by her lonesome."

"Ah."

"And think about things."

"Yes, I see."

"She's a deep person, you know."

"I'll bet she is."

"If you give me your name, I'll tell her you called."

"Oh, that's all right. I'll try her again tomorrow."

"You don't want to leave a name, sir?"

"Let's make it a surprise."

She shrugged. "If you say so, sir." She closed the door.

The gazebo. The backyard. Most of the city blocks had alleys.

I walked my horse down to the end of the block and turned left. The day birds were crying out in sharp bursts, lamenting the dying of light; the night birds were hailing the darkness.

I found an alley and took it.

There were three houses on the block where Jenny Rice lived and four houses on the other side of the alley. The backs of these houses looked huge in the gloom, lower windows alight, dogs and kids and cats and husbands being called in for supper. I tied my horse's reins to a nearby branch and let him munch away on some grass as I tried to get a better look at the Rice place.

Several oak trees screened the Rice backyard from the alley. You could see between them, but you had to look hard.

The gazebo was small and white and sat in the center of a vast plain of rich green prairie grass, recently mown and smelling beautiful. Fireflies looped and dove through the last of dusk.

At first, I couldn't make her out in there. The shadows were heavy and she was so small, she vanished inside them.

But then she moved to pick something up and I glimpsed her. She wore something dark, which didn't help.

I bent down and walked between the lower branches of the oak trees and came out on the lawn.

If she saw me, she didn't let on.

I walked toward the gazebo. I tried to move in such an obvious way that there was no doubt I was here on a friendly mission.

I was about halfway there when somebody said, "Hold it, son, 'less you want a backside full of buckshot."

He came from behind me. He walked around me so he could face me and so I could see his rifle. It was a nice one, a repeater.

"Bess signaled me you might be comin'," he said.

"And Bess would be the woman who answered the door?"

"That would be Bess, yes, sir. And Bess would be my wife. Yes, sir."

I suspected he was probably the same age as his wife but he looked older. White fringe of hair on the very black head. No hair at all up top.

"I just came to see Miss Rice."

"She be busy."

I tried to look past him to the gazebo, which was some distance away. "She always have an armed guard, does she?"

"Ever since the trial. Lots of folks in these parts liked Mr. Donald. They hate her for a-killin' him."

"Did you like Mr. Donald?"

"He was jes' about the nicest white man I ever did know. And my Bess'll tell you the same thing."

"So she's afraid somebody'll try and kill her."

"It's possible, yes, sir. In these days, *anythin'* is possible."

"I'd have to agree with you there."

A sweet contralto voice called out. "Who is it, Fogarty?"

"Some man to see you. Looks like he done brung you a present."

I'd forgotten about the package in my hand.

"Who is he?" she said.

I spoke before he could. "I have malaria, Miss Rice. You took care of a lot of friends of mine in the hospital. And we just got up a gift to show you our appreciation."

I was careful not to say that *I* had been in the hospital.

"Well, isn't that sweet? Let him come up, Fogarty. I'm sure he's all right."

"You don't mind, Miss Rice, I be doin' my job and fol-lowin' right along behind him with this here rifle."

And he did, too.

I took the two steps up into the gazebo. She pointed to an empty rocking chair identical to the one she sat in. At least, it seemed to be identical. It was dark.

I sat down.

The man still had the rifle on me. "He doesn't stay here all the time, does he?"

She smiled. "Not unless you want him to."

"Sure, maybe he could sit on my lap and I could rock him."

"There's no need for sarcasm. He's simply protecting me. People seem to think I'm this helpless butterfly." It was odd the way she said it, and it told me something about her. Most folks delivering that line would've made fun of it, meaning that they weren't helpless butterflies at all. But the way Jenny Rice said it—with no humor in it at all—I got the impression that that was how she saw herself, too.

She said, "I had rheumatic fever when I was a child and nearly died. I spent a good deal of my time indoors and in bed. I've never fully recovered. You have to be careful with me, Mr. Lamont. I break very easily. That's all Fogarty is worried about, that I'll be all right. He's been in the family for nearly fifty years and he knows how sensitive I can be."

Lucky him, I thought. A little bit of the South right here in Wisconsin. All they needed was some drooping Spanish moss, a few more pillars holding up their front roof, and a handful of darkies working the land that ran behind the estate.

I didn't like her, I didn't like her would-be mansion, and I suddenly felt sorry for the old gink with the rifle. He should've turned it on her long ago.

"Would you be ever so kind as to get us some cool tea, Fogarty?"

"Yes' ma'am."

"And be sure to bring the lace napkins."

"Yes, ma'am."

"The *fawn-colored* lace napkins, Fogarty. Not the blue-colored lace ones you brought last time."

"Yes, ma'am."

"And please be sure to make the tea *cool,* not tepid, the way it was last time."

"Yes, ma'am."

"And one more thing. Please don't come sneaking up on us in the dark. Clear your throat or something. We don't want to be ambushed, now do we, Mr. Lamont?" She had a silly little laugh, a spoiled little girl's laugh, and I didn't like that, either.

After her man-boy was gone, she said, "My father brought him up from Georgia before the war. He trained him personally. I could never train him. You have to be stern with them and I'm afraid I'm just too kind."

"Yes, I can see that."

"Now, relax, Mr. Lamont. I want you to feel at home."

"You know who I am."

"I saw you at the hospital one day. How is your malaria doing?"

"I'm glad you mentioned the hospital. Some of us got together and bought you a gift for all the work you did there."

"Well, good Lord, now isn't that nice of you?"

We spent the next five minutes unwrapping the gift, remarking on the gift, gushing about how malaria seemed to bring out just the nicest side of the "local folk," as she called them, and how she was so glad to find out that those same local folk didn't resent her presence in the hospital.

"You know, there are people who just seem to resent elegant ladies of my position and wealth. As my father always said, it's just that little green-eyed demon called jealousy. He was a believer in the natural order—that some are born to lead and some are born to follow. And that's just the way things are."

I was going to mention that the czar in Russia had run into some trouble recently for expressing similar beliefs. But I decided she probably wasn't much interested in history.

As for her being elegant—how could I disagree? I'd never really seen her before up close. But sitting so properly in her chair in the gazebo, a white organdy gown and a wrap enfolding her slender body, she certainly looked beautiful enough. I could see why a shy and decent man like Donald Wylie would have been taken with her.

"Where is he with that tea? My father always used a stopwatch with him. And if Fogarty was late, he got a beating."

"Gosh, I guess I was under the impression that the slavery issue had pretty much been decided."

The nasty little laugh again, the one that told me how stupid I—and everybody else—was. "Why, it's not slavery, Mr. Lamont. Fogarty gets paid three dollars a week, has a nice little place fixed up for him over the stable, and can come and go as he pleases. As long as all his work is done."

"I guess there are different kinds of slavery."

"Meaning what exactly?"

"Meaning three dollars a week is a *form* of slavery."

She sighed. "Have you ever heard him pass gas? Or belch when he's eating? Have you ever smelled him after he hasn't bathed for two weeks? Or caught him peeking in the bedroom window to catch a glimpse of you naked? Or heard him ridicule you to the other people who work here? My father—God rest his soul—may not have been an ideal employer, Mr. Lamont. But Fogarty is hardly the ideal *employee*, either."

It was then that Fogarty, somewhere in the gloom, cleared his throat.

We spent another five minutes with her assessing the situation: the tea was cooler than last time, but still not as cool as she'd hoped (but, being the gallant girl she was, she'd drink it anyway), and the napkins, while tan, were not the lace napkins she'd asked for and hadn't he been awfully close to the gazebo before he'd cleared his throat and announced his presence.

"I'm sorry if you heard anything that was hurtful to your pride, Fogarty. About passing gas or peeking in my window. But our guest Mr. Lamont here was implying that I was some sort of sadist employer who spent her time tormenting you. And that isn't the case at all, is it?"

"No, ma'am."

"In fact, if I were to discharge you tonight, you would have noplace else to go, would you?"

"No, ma'am."

"And you'd plead with me to stay, wouldn't you?"

"Yes' ma'am. I shore enough would."

The thing was, you might get the idea that he was just being a dutiful man-boy, saying what his white-lady boss wanted and expected him to say. But he sounded sincere. And when she mentioned firing him, he sounded scared.

"Does that satisfy you, Mr. Lamont?"

I wasn't quite sure what to say. Maybe after I left she'd take it all out on poor Fogarty.

I decided now would be a good time to get on to the topic I was here to discuss. "I think my brother may have known this Susan Baxter, Miss Lamont. I'm trying to tie up some loose ends with his estate and all. We have a farm and some land back in Ohio. I wondered if Donald had told you where she was from."

She said, "Fogarty, go back to the house."

"Yes, miss."

"And don't come back till I call for you."

"Yes, miss."

"And I mean, *no sneaking up to eavesdrop.*"

"Yes, ma'am."

"That's another one of his nicer habits, isn't it, Fogarty? He's a born snoop. Right, Fogarty?"

"Yes, ma'am."

We watched him walk, toting his rifle, back toward the house and the lights. There were night birds and the faint play of music from downtown and a lonely clip-clop of a horse on a dark road somewhere nearby.

When he was out of earshot, she leaned to me and said:

"I can't believe you've come to my house to talk about the woman who destroyed my life."

"I've tried everybody else. Nobody seems to know where she went."

"She lives in Daly City."

"Not anymore," I lied. "That's why I came here. I thought maybe Donald had said something about where she lived originally. Maybe after all that's happened, she's gone back there."

"I'm sure I wouldn't know."

I sighed. "I see."

"I really resent this, Mr. Lamont. After all I've been through—to come here and ask me questions about her—"

"Did you ever actually see them together?"

"See who together?"

"Donald and Susan Baxter."

"Of course I did."

"It must've been difficult for you."

"It was, very much so."

I sat back in the rocking chair and waited. Sometimes silence made people anxious and talkative.

"I saw them together twice."

"I see."

"Just as I testified in court."

"Ah, yes, the trial."

"I was so jealous, I took complete leave of my senses. I—I can't even remember shooting Donald."

I wondered if she *had* shot Donald. Easy for Jed to do it and then hand her the gun. A lady of her delicate sensibilities might well shrink from violence. Pass me the smelling salts, darlin'. Besides, someone had told me that she grew up in a Quaker household. Violence was shunned by most Quakers. I'd met a few, and while her folks might very well have been Quaker, Jenny Rice didn't appear to have the same views as her folks. She had a Negro manservant whom she treated like dirt and she was involved in the violent death of a man she professed to have loved. No, not very Quaker at all.

"You must've been quite angry."

"More than angry, Mr. Lamont. Angry and hurt and humiliated. I'm just glad my father wasn't alive to see it." She brought a lacy handkerchief up to her eyes and lightly dabbed at them, then sighed. "Thank goodness I have a place to go for all my confessions."

"Oh?"

"My journal. I write down all my thoughts in it."

Too bad she hadn't kept her thoughts of violence to Donald Wylie as just ink and paper.

One thing I had to give her—she was a pretty damned good actress. On the stand, at least the day I saw her, she'd been pale, withered, and pathetic. And at the hospital, a soft-spoken saint too humble to even wear her halo. But tonight she was the belle of the plantation—full of herself and full of shit.

"How did we ever get on this subject, anyway?" she said. "I really don't want to discuss it."

"And you won't have to," I said. I stood up. "I need to be leaving. I just wanted to make sure you got our gift."

"Why, you're leaving so soon, Mr. Lamont. I thought that perhaps you'd enjoy another glass of tea."

"No, thank you, miss. With my malaria and all, I tire easily."

"I so much appreciate this gift."

"It's been my pleasure, ma'am."

She allowed me the honor of kissing her hand. I was

surprised she didn't offer me the equal honor of kissing her ass. The way poor old Fogarty had to do every ninety seconds or so.

I didn't go far, just out to the alley and several yards down, where there was a sturdy pin oak in the process of full bloom. My tree-climbing days were well behind me so it took me a while to shinny and crawl up the damned thing. I ripped the crotch of my trousers, tore off a chunk of fingernail, and scraped the side of my face getting into place.

Once I settled in, though, it was nice. I was up high enough for a nice view of the sleepy neighborhood. The half-moon painted everything silver and shadow. Sweet swift housecats prowled the backyards while back-porch dogs snored peacefully into the early summer darkness. Somewhere a mother sang a lullaby to her baby; a grandpa in a nightshirt stood on his porch smoking his last pipe for the day and inhaling the scent of all those lovely wan flowers.

I sat up in the crook of a tree, the way I used to as a kid whenever I played pirates, pretending I was up on the captain's walk searching the horizon of sea for a British ship.

My ass went first. It usually does. Some people lose circulation in their arms and some in their legs when they're in cramped quarters. With me, it's always my ass. I'm sure there's a good medical reason for this—one that involves those long Latin words you see in medical dictionaries—but I have no idea what it is. My ass went to sleep and then my eyes started to blink. I was getting tired.

Maybe I was wrong. Maybe nothing was going to happen. Maybe she wasn't suspicious at all. And maybe she wouldn't use her telephone—one of the few in town—to call her lover Jed Wylie. And lover was the right word. That's the only way these things ever worked. Jed could've talked her into this scheme only if he'd taken the place of his brother in her affections. Love or lust or whatever to call it was the only feeling strong enough to inspire this kind of loyalty. I'll pretend I murdered him and I'll risk standing it if you'll just tell me you love me. A small price to pay.

What she didn't realize—what they never realize until it's too late—was that Jed couldn't leave her alive. She'd always represent the ultimate threat to him. She couldn't ever be tried for Donald's murder again. But he could. And that made her, for him, the most dangerous person alive.

I must've been up in the tree a good hour and a half before she left the house.

She went to the stable and got herself a horse and got him all saddled up and took off riding fast. Gone was the wispy plantation mistress. This was hard prairie woman here. She'd thrown that saddle around quickly and expertly. Fogarty hadn't needed to help her. She was an interesting combination of roles, Jenny was.

I got my own horse and followed, hanging back as far as a quarter mile at some flatland points.

She followed the moonsilver river. We passed a small hobo jungle where the river swung wide adjacent to some railroad tracks, a gypsy camp, and a small crude stone grotto to the Blessed Virgin. Pioneers had built and left such grottos all along the trail as they'd pushed west—good luck for themselves, they'd hoped, and good luck for those who came after, who knelt by the grotto and prayed.

She met him at a shack in some dense timber. It had likely been built by the railroad thirty years ago when they headed for Wyoming and Colorado.

I ground-tied my horse and cut a wide arc on the timbered hill above the shack, the scent of pine needles so heavy it was half-intoxicating. A raccoon by the side of the trail gave me an irritated look, as if he wanted to see the ticket that gave me the right to be in this here woods, and then bounced away. A possum scurried in front of me so fast I didn't see it until too late. And then I stumbled into some heavy off-path vegetation, grabbing a mossy tree to keep from falling.

They stood in a small clearing in front of the cabin. They probably didn't want to go inside. Too many snakes and rabbits, too cloying a smell. This would be the outhouse of choice for a million of God's smallest creatures.

"He thought he was so clever," she said.

"He always does," Jed said. He didn't sound happy.

"I think he's figured it all out, Jed. I know you don't want to hear that. But I think that's what's going on here. He put the whole thing together."

All the plantation mannerisms—the arch verbosity, especially—were gone. She spoke plain hard prairie talk.

"Maybe I should just give him all the bank money."

"Part of that's mine, remember? We agreed to an even split. And then we leave town separately and meet in Chicago in two weeks? Or don't you remember our plan?"

So there it was. The kind of plan that always sounds sensible when you're caught up in the fleshy tangle of lust. How easy it all is. Shoot him in the back. Stick up the bank. Flee to Chicago. So easy.

Yet, as the time approaches, and the blinding heat of bed begins to fade, you begin to see the flaws in your plan. You see all the ways it can go wrong.

"Jed?"

"What?"

"You didn't answer me."

"Answer you about what?"

"I asked if you'd forgotten our plan."

"No, of course I haven't."

"You haven't touched me for over two weeks."

"For God's sake, Jenny, what the hell do you want me to do? Have sex with you in the middle of the street like some dog?"

"When we first started out, you would have."

"Fuck," he said.

"I've asked you not to use that word."

"Oh, yes, I forgot. We have to watch our language when we're sipping mint juleps on the porch, don't we?"

She said, quietly, "I wish I'd never gotten into all this."

"Great," he said. "That's all I need to hear. First you tell me that sonofabitch Lamont is nosing into our business. And now you tell me that you wish you'd never gotten involved in the whole thing."

"I only did it because I thought you loved me," she said miserably.

"I *do* love you."

"Then could you show it? Could you take me in your arms and hold me? You've avoided touching me since I came here tonight."

"It's just I've got so damned much on my mind."

"I hope you're still planning to run away with me. That was our agreement."

She had to be scaring him. He was smart. He knew what he was hearing—a scared and perhaps remorseful woman, one who could easily be coerced into confessing by a smart and patient man like Chief Pekins.

He took her in his arms and then kissed her tenderly.

•   •   •

There was only one saloon left open when I got back to town. One of Pekins's boys was rounding up drunks. It was a clean little place and they meant to keep it that way.

I was restless. I had everything I needed now. For my satisfaction, anyway. But it wouldn't be enough for Pekins. I still had some work to do where he was concerned.

I played poker till nearly three. The game was low stakes but interesting. Two old boys were mad at each other over previous nights of playing. Tonight they were trying to destroy each other.

In bed, I lay awake for at least an hour. I wondered when it had changed for Jed. The killing. We'd always been strict about that. No violence. It ended for me just the other day. At least I had the excuse of trying to save a life. But Jed had turned killer, and with his own brother. I wondered what did it, what pushed him over.

They say you learn more as you get older. That's not always a blessing.

SIXTEEN

"YOU LOOK LIKE shit," Stodla said.

"Thanks."

"Malaria?"

"Couldn't sleep."

"Oh."

Stodla was eating one of his enormous breakfasts when I got down to the café in the morning. "You know what I always do when I can't sleep?"

"What?"

"Try'n remember all the girls I slept with."

"That would sure be a lot of them," I said. Every place we went, there was always a woman—and some of them damned good-looking—who wanted to try on somebody Stodla's size.

"You should try it, Lamont."

"Haven't slept with half the women you have."

"You've done all right for yourself. Don't kid me." Then he looked up. "He's lookin' for somebody."

"Who is?"

"Pekins."

I'm not sure why but my first thought was that Pekins was looking for me. I was right.

"Morning, gentlemen," he said. His arm was still in a sling but he managed to look dapper anyway.

"Morning," Stodla said heartily.

"Lamont, I'm going to go in the back there and have a couple of cups of coffee. Why don't you wander back there when you finish up your breakfast?" Pekins asked.

"Any particular reason?"

"Yeah. Because I said so." He nodded good-bye to us and then walked to the back, stopping at various tables to do some politicking. An elected office like his, you had to keep your public very happy.

"Wonder what he wants," Stodla said.

"So do I."

"He ain't a bad guy. Jed likes him."

I wonder how *much* Jed likes him, I thought. But then dismissed the notion. Pekins might be his brother-in-law, but he wouldn't be a part of Jed's scheme. He was strictly straight and narrow. That was his pride, the incorruptible lawman.

"You get in any trouble, you just let Jed know. He can help you out. Him and Pekins there're good friends."

"Well," I said, finished with my eggs, toast, and coffee. "Might as well see what it's all about."

"Remember about Jed."

"I will. Thanks, Stodla."

"Good luck, kid."

I smiled. He hadn't called me kid in a lot of long years. I used to resent it. Now there was something nice and pa-

ternal about it. Poor Stodla. In his way, he was as much a
victim as any of the people he'd ever taken advantage of.

I walked to the back and found Pekins.

"You keep late hours," he said.

"I do?"

"Calling on respectable citizens at all hours."

"Jenny Rice."

"That's right, Lamont," Pekins said. "Jenny Rice." Then,
"How's your coffee this morning?"

"A little bitter. Not as good as usual."

"That's what I was thinking. Must've been Merle this
morning instead of Tolliver."

I wasn't familiar with the staff the way Pekins was.

"He puts too much salt in it."

"I see."

"Merle, I mean. Not Tolliver. Tolliver makes it just right.
You can always tell a Tolliver cup of coffee."

"That sounds like an advertising slogan."

He smiled. "You know, I believe it does. 'You can always tell a Tolliver cup of coffee.'" Then, "That was a stupid fucking thing you did last night."

"Yeah, it probably was."

"She told me she's not going to lodge any kind of formal complaint but she sure will the next time you go out
there and bother her."

She wouldn't lodge *any* kind of complaint. Not ever.
Neither she nor Jed could stand the scrutiny.

I was tempted to tell Pekins the whole thing, just spread
it all out on the table like a map.

But it was too soon. I needed more. Jed could mollify
him and turn it all back on me.

"She says she's afraid of you."

"Yes, she did seem sort of frail. I suppose I spooked her but I sure didn't mean to."

"You need to let this thing go, Lamont. With your brother, I mean. A bunch of stupid bank robbers made a sweep down from Canada and fucked up a bank robbery, nothing more to it than that. Your brother was a nice young man. I liked him a lot. Was going to ask him if he wanted to be a policeman, in fact."

"Really?"

"You bet. He was smart and decent and levelheaded. You don't find many youngsters in their early twenties like that."

I formed a picture of Paul in a policeman's uniform. A right smart picture it was, too. He would've made a good cop.

"Thanks for telling me that."

He sipped his coffee. "Shit. That damned Merle. I come over here for my morning coffee and he salts the hell out of it." Then, "I don't know what the hell she had to do with it, anyway."

"Who're you talking about?"

"Jenny Rice. How could she've helped you with the bank robbers?"

He had asked one of those questions I had no logical answer to, not unless I told him everything.

"I wanted to bring her that gift from the patients at the hospital."

"What gift?"

I told him.

"She didn't mention that."

"Sure. Why else would I go out there? She's helped a lot of people at the hospital."

"That's the kind of woman she is." Then, "Well, whyever

you went over there, she doesn't want you coming around anymore."

"So I gather."

"She deserves some peace, after the trial and all. She's not a strong woman and the combination of losing her man and then going insane and killing him—" He shook his head. "I just want to make sure she has some peace and quiet."

"I'll stay away from her. I promise."

"Good." He smiled. "And don't forget what I said about leaving town soon, too. You actually make me kind of nervous, sort of hovering over everything here. It's all closed up, Mr. Lamont. The whole case."

I stood up. Put out my hand. He shook it. "Don't go thinking I've got a weak grip, Lamont. I don't. It's just that my regular hand is in a cast at the moment."

Actually, I'd thought his grip was pretty damned strong. The good hand must really have been a honey.

When I got out into the sunny day, a nap sounded good to me. An hour in bed and I'd be able to appreciate the fine summer day. I went up to my room.

Susan Baxter was waiting there for me.

With a gun.

SEVENTEEN

"SOMETHING'S GOING ON."

"Yeah, you're sitting in my room holding a gun on me."

"This thing?" She pitched it on the bed. "It isn't even loaded. What do I know about guns?"

"So what're you doing with it?"

"I thought maybe you were in on it with him. I thought maybe you'd turn on me."

I went over to the top drawer of the bureau where I kept my bottle of whiskey. "You want a drink?"

"I could use one."

"Maybe you'll make more sense then."

I found two glasses and filled them halfway. When I handed a glass to her, she said, "You're not in on it with him?"

"In on what?"

"The whole setup. Bringing the gang down from Canada. Shooting Donald. Everything."

"What made you so willing to talk all of a sudden?"

She sipped her whiskey. There was a breeze through the window. The curtain filled and fluttered. She closed her eyes to appreciate the moment. "I never should've trusted the bastard. Remember how he ran out on me in Missouri that time?"

"I thought it was Minnesota."

"Minnesota was another time."

"And wasn't there something in Montana—?"

"The fucker," she said. "The fucker." Her face was suddenly rash-red with anger. "It doesn't say a whole hell of a lot for me that I'd trust him again."

She had on a tiny blue hat that matched her dark blue traveling suit. She looked fetching as hell.

"People never seem to learn with Jed," I said. "I don't know why. It's like he hypnotizes them or something. Hell, look at Stodla. He's left Stodla holding the bag two or three times and Stodla never seems to mind. Jed gives him some excuse and he buys it."

"Well, I'm not buying it. Not this time."

"You going to the law?"

She glanced over at me and laughed. "Me? Go to the law? How could I? I was part of it. They'd never believe that I wasn't part of the murder, too."

"You didn't know he was going to kill Donald?"

"All I knew was that he paid me five hundred dollars to pretend that Donald and I were having an affair on the side, Donald being engaged to Jenny Rice. Never a mention of anybody being killed. I just figured it was some con Jed was pushing. You know how he always came up with those brilliant ideas that never amounted to shit. Well, this sounded like another one of them. I asked for my money up front and when I got it, I lost all interest. It was just if anybody asked me if I was having an affair with Donald, I was to say yes. That was the whole thing."

"Maybe the law would believe you."

"Oh, sure, with a record like mine."

"You were never involved in murder before."

"No, but I've been involved in everything else." She killed the last of her drink and stared out the window. "Never got around to having a husband or a kid or a house. That was always my plan. Work the con for a few years and build up a little nest egg and retire and live like everybody else. But somehow it never came to pass."

"You're not exactly ancient."

"Not when I've got my clothes on. Naked is another story. Naked I'm going fast, Bryce. And it won't be long before it starts to show in my face and neck. Then it'll be all over. There're already a lot of younger girls working all the cons we did. I was on a riverboat last year and I think there were more girls working cons than there were passengers. Good-looking, smart girls, too. Hard for me to compete with much longer." Then, "I don't suppose you'd want to sleep with me."

I smiled. She wanted reassurance and it was sort of sad and endearing at the same time. She hadn't taken any prisoners back in her prime. She'd broken hearts coast to coast and now she was asking for a little mercy herself.

"I don't look all that good with *my* clothes off, either," I said.

"You look just fine, Bryce."

"Tell me that after you see my beer gut." Then, "C'mon, let's take our clothes off and make each other sick."

She giggled and it was a sweet girly sound that was just right for the moment and then we tumbled into bed and started kissing and fumbling around and fooling around and then we were making love and I felt closer to her than I ever thought possible and I think she felt the same way, too, because she'd tear up every once in a while and I'd kiss her wet face dry again.

We took a good nap. I needed it and apparently she did, too. We slept till five. Finding a good sleep partner is harder than finding a good lover. You need somebody whose body shapes itself the way yours does during sleep. She worked just fine. We slept as one.

When I woke up, she was sitting, dressed, in a chair by the window. She was drinking my whiskey.

"You all right?" I asked.

"I came here so you would know I didn't have anything to do with your brother's death."

"I appreciate it."

"It's time somebody stopped him, Bryce."

"Yeah, it is."

She smiled sadly. "I keep this kind of diary. I looked back and read what I wrote about you when I first met you. I had a crush on you."

"And vice versa." I thought of Susan Baxter's diary, then thought of the terrible diary of Jenny Rice. Here was Susan, a woman of the world, with an innocent crush. Jenny Rice's diary couldn't be more different.

"Really?"

"Hell, yes. You're a beautiful woman." Then, "She keeps a diary, too. Calls it a journal."

"Who?"

"Jenny Rice."

"How do you know that?"

"She told me."

Another sip of whiskey. "Bet she wrote all the same kinds of crazy bullshit about Jed that I did."

"She'd really have to love him to go along with what she did."

"Donald was kind of a prick."

"Never met the man."

"Kind of prissy. Real cheap. Always giving Jed these lectures about morality and the family honor. I imagine Jed had a good time killing him."

"I imagine he did."

She read my mind. "I'm real sorry about your brother, Bryce."

I nodded. "That's all I give a shit about in this. The kid being killed and all."

"That's why I say he's got to be stopped now. Finally."

"Yeah.

"My train leaves in two hours," she said. "I just wish I could find him so I could slap his face."

"Just stay away from him. Get your train and get the hell out of here."

She put her drink down and came over to the bed. "I don't want to get undressed again but I'll give you a blow job if you want it."

"Nah. I appreciate the offer, but I'm fine."

"You sure?"

"Yeah." I was tired again. It didn't feel like a malaria attack, just the fatigue that went with a malaria attack.

"You look like you could use some more sleep."

"Yeah, I guess I could."

"Well, I've got a nice novel I'm reading, so I guess I'll just go read it in the train depot."

"Sorry I'm so worn out."

She gave me a long and sweet kiss. I had more feelings for her than I'd realized.

"So long, Bryce," she said from the door.

"So long." Then she was gone.

EIGHTEEN

THE RAIN WAS bitter and hot and I was kneeling next to the kid's gravestone and asking him to forgive me. Then the rain started to rip my face and I suddenly felt like a leper.

Then there was the knocking. It was loud and I couldn't figure out where it was coming from. I was in a graveyard. There shouldn't have been any knocking.

And then somebody was shaking me. I had a hard time waking up. I wanted the kid to understand how sorry I was.

". . . wants you right away," someone was saying.

Somebody was lighting the lantern on my nightstand. The man shaking me had on one of Pekins's snappy uniforms. He looked to be half Mex. I'd never seen him before.

". . . so you come with me," he said.

The other peace officer was rounding up my clothes and shoes. Just as I was sitting up on the edge of the bed, he threw them at me. I needed a smoke before I did anything.

I got one fired up and sat there rubbing my head and face and saying, "What the hell's going on?"

"He said not to say nothing to you," the half Mex said.

"I take it you mean Pekins."

"Yeah," he said. "Pekins."

I started climbing into my clothes. "What time is it?"

"Three fifteen."

"Shit," I said. "I should still be asleep."

"Just hurry up."

"I wish I knew what the hell was going on."

"I'm going on ahead," the half Mex said.

"Tell him we'll be right along," the other one said to him, then turned to me and added, "Hurry up, can't you?"

"I have fucking malaria, all right?" I said.

He grinned. "Guess what, asshole. I've had malaria since I was ten years old. You think I use it as an excuse every time I get tired?"

I had to admit, that was a pretty good one. Nothing much I could say to it.

All those warm, snug people sleeping in their warm, snug beds. That was all I could think of as we passed the darkened houses on our way to somewhere only Pekins and his men knew about.

"You've really had malaria since you were ten?" I asked.

"Yeah."

"You still get the bad stuff every couple days?"

"Not always. Sometimes it'll go away for a while."

"How long?"

"Months. Went near a year once. You just got to keep taking your medicine all the time."

"You ever get used to the taste?"

He laughed. "Not so's you'd notice."

His laugh encouraged me. "What's going on with Pekins?"

"I can't say. So don't ask me anymore, all right?"

The night sounds—insects, birds, electrical poles, distant trains—sounded sort of eerie to my sleepy ears. This was a world I knew nothing about. Usually when I was up this late, I was drunk and didn't hear any of it.

Dirt streets. Bicycles parked in front yards. Sleepy dogs watching us from shadowy porches. Cats stalking and prowling.

The blocks got longer and the houses bigger. We were past all the small white frame houses with the picket fences. Now the mansions and estates started. Cupolas and high dormers and even a few minarets were outlined against the starry night. One Victorian house stood alone on a hill, looking like something the *Strand Detective Magazine* would run on its cover along with an Arthur Conan Doyle story. Sherlock Holmes was popular in prison.

I saw the dead man before the copper did. He lay sprawled in the sanded and oiled roadway, facedown, arms flung wide.

"This must be it, huh?" I said.

"What're you talking about?"

"This must be what Pekins wanted me to see?"

He squinted into the gloom. The nearest streetlamp was a few hundred yards away. He apparently still couldn't see what I saw. "You got good eyes, mister."

"The guy in the street? Facedown?"

He walked a little faster and then said, "Oh. Him."

"Yeah. Him."

The first thing he did when we reached the man was kick him in the butt. Not hard, not mean.

"He's dead," I said.

"Dead drunk, you mean."

"He isn't dead?"

"Hell, no. That's Mr. Peyton. He owns the paint store. Inhales those fumes all day and then gets all liquored up three, four nights a week. About half the time he don't even make it this far. Sleeps it off in the street and then sneaks home around dawn and his old lady works him over with a broom. One time she got so bad we had to keep him in a cell just so she couldn't get to him. I don't blame her, though. I had an old man like him and I tell ya, it sure ain't no way to grow up."

He went over and got Peyton under the arms and lifted him up and threw him over his shoulder. He wasn't very big as peace officers went but then neither was Peyton.

We went two blocks west and dumped the drunk on his own porch. He made a loud noise when he hit the floor. A lamp bloomed in the back of the house.

"I don't want to hear any of this," he said. "Let's get the hell out of here."

We'd just made the street when a big woman in a man's bathrobe came out with a broom in her hand and started pounding on Peyton, who was still sprawled where we'd thrown him.

"He ever remember you bringing him home?"

"Not very often."

"Wish I could forget things that way sometimes," I said, thinking of my brother. "My curse is that I always remember."

"Yeah," he said, "sometimes that's the worst thing of all—having a memory."

We walked back to the main road.

On the way the hearse from the funeral home came by. It looked shiny black and very theatrical in the moonlight.

You half-expected a ghoul was inside and ready to jump out. I wondered what the hell was going on.

Our destination was Jenny Rice's place. It was all lit up and Pekins was there and there must've been thirty, forty other people, too, mostly—judging from the fact they were dressed in nightclothes—neighbors. They looked like most people at scenes like this. They wanted to know and they didn't want to know.

Pekins was on the porch, talking to the manservant Fogarty, when I walked up to him.

"You know Mr. Fogarty?" Pekins said.

"Met him the other night."

Fogarty and I nodded hello.

"What's going on?" I said.

"You want to tell him, Mr. Fogarty? You were here and heard it all."

Fogarty gulped. "Yes, sir. I heard it all, all right. And I sure wish I hadn't."

"Heard what?" I asked.

"When Miss Jenny, she shot that Baxter woman and then kilt herself."

"Oh, shit," I said. "Are you sure?"

"Well," Pekins said, "we've got two corpses in there. The Baxter woman took two bullets in the chest and Jenny Rice took one bullet to the temple. The powder residue on her gun hand is easy to see. So I'd say it's pretty self-explanatory, especially given their history."

"He set it up," I said.

"Who?" Pekins said.

I pushed past him and went inside. Went through the vestibule, peeked in the parlor, and went on down to the library. That's where they were, in front of the dead, dark fireplace. Jenny Rice on the left, Susan Baxter on the right.

I knelt down next to Susan, touched her face. Waxy. Cold. Dead. She wouldn't have to worry about getting old now, watch her looks go, that slow sadness that only true beauties can ever know. I was glad we'd made love and had some laughs. I'd always liked her.

I looked at Jenny Rice. Didn't touch her. Didn't want to.

I went upstairs quickly. She seemed to have three bed-rooms. Each one was carefully composed. There was a regal one, a little girl one, and a modern, rather austere one. I went through every drawer in every one of the rooms, but couldn't find it. I was just checking out the closet in the little girl bedroom when Pekins said, "If you'll tell me what you're looking for, maybe I can help you find it."

"Ashtray."

"Interesting place to look for an ashtray. A bedroom closet."

I turned and faced him. "She was a good woman."

"I take it you mean Baxter."

"Yeah."

"And when you said, 'He set this up,' I take it you mean my brother-in-law, Jed Wylie."

"Yeah."

"Meaning what exactly?"

"Meaning this wasn't a murder-suicide. It was a double homicide."

He looked doubtful. "I see. And you can prove that?"

"I can sure as hell try."

"He won't like it."

"You really think I give a damn?"

"What if *I* don't like it?"

I sighed. "Somebody has to stop him."

"You make him sound like a terrible man."

"He *is* a terrible man. I never realized how terrible until I got here tonight."

He looked at me awhile and said, "Be careful, Lamont, or you're going to get both of our dicks cut off."

Then he turned and walked away.

NINETEEN

I SLEPT LATE the next morning. Couldn't help it. Couldn't wake up.

Stodla woke me up by jimmying my door and walking in. He pulled up a chair and sat down next to me.

"Sure glad I ain't got that shit. I guess mosquitoes just naturally don't like me."

"What time is it?"

"Around three."

"God."

"You gettin' up?"

"Yeah."

He moved his chair back so I could sit on the side of the bed. Sunshine made the floor warm where I put my feet. I felt very old and very young—old man–sick and kid-sick. I was headed for a spell of it again.

"Jed send you over here?"

"Yeah."

"Figures."

He got out one of my cigarettes and put it between my lips and struck a kitchen match for me.

"He just wanted you to know that he's gonna do somethin' nice for Sally."

"Sally. Yeah. That was her name. She used so many different names over the years I actually forgot her real name."

"Anyway, he's gonna take care of her. You know, since that little bitch killed her and all."

"You think Jenny Rice killed her, huh, Stodla?"

"Hell, I know so."

"Jed tell you that, did he?"

"Jed and the whole town. Pretty obvious what happened, Bryce."

"Is it?"

I got up and walked over to the basin. The water was warm. What the hell. I didn't feel up to walking down the hall. A spell was definitely coming.

I splashed water on my face. When I was done, I used the water to shave.

"Jed said he hears you've got some other ideas."

"Oh?"

"He hears you don't think it was the Rice woman who did it."

I got my beard lathered and started shaving in the dim mirror. A fly played nuisance all the time I stroked away. He'd land on my forehead, my elbow, my knuckle. I guess he thought we were buddies.

"He's got a nice way about him."

"Oh?" Stodla says.

"He kills a woman and then he offers to pay for her burial. Only Jed could come up with something like that."

"You shouldn't ought to say things like that, Bryce. He

feels real bad about Sally. You know, they got together a few times over the years. I think he really liked her."

I watched him in the mirror. "He probably did. Until he had to kill her."

Stodla shook his head, sad-like. "You and I sure see Jed different."

"We sure do."

"You ever seen him around little kids? He loves little kids. Now no man who's that nice to little kids could be bad."

"If you say so."

He hesitated, played with the brim of his dusty hat. "You push him on this, Bryce, he's gonna be real pissed."

"Figures."

"*Real* pissed, if you get my point."

I turned and looked at him. "He killed those two women, Stodla. You know it and I know it. The difference is, I'll admit it to myself and you won't."

"He just couldn't have, Bryce. He couldn't have. It just wouldn't be in him." He looked and sounded sick. I think he was scared that he'd bumped up against something that he couldn't move out of his way. Jed had finally done something here that not even Stodla could deny. "He cared about her, Bryce."

"You know, the funny thing is," I said, turning back to the mirror and my shaving, "is that I believe he did. He doesn't kill just anybody. Just people he feels he has to. I even believe he regrets it. I don't think he's one of those stone-cold killers who enjoys what he does. He's just a businessman who cuts his losses when he needs to. I imagine he might even have cried about what he did. And I'm sure when he kneels down next to Sally's grave, every prayer he says will be sincere. It'll be like somebody else killed her."

Stodla sighed. "I sure wish I wouldn't've come up here."

"That's because you know I'm telling you the truth."

He stood up. "I wish you coulda seen them welts my pa used to put on my back with his strap. Or the way he busted up my left arm in three places. Or the way he used to beat up my ma so bad she died one night. Jed and his folks, they took me away from that. They gave me a place to live and food to eat and they even managed to see I got through seventh grade. You know many people who'd do that for some dumb-pecker plow jockey?"

Stodla hadn't looked at me till now. "And Jed protected me. Anybody ever picked on me in any way, he'd stand up for me. And if they picked on me again, he'd beat the shit out of them. I know how much you loved your brother, Bryce. But you can't seem to understand how much I love *my* brother. He's my brother, Jed is. Good as blood; maybe even stronger than blood because we never argued the way blood kin sometimes do. You never understood that, did you, Bryce?"

And he was right. I never did, not until this moment. I knew that Stodla appreciated what Jed and his family had done for him. But I never realized in a direct, emotional way what their bond meant to Stodla.

"You're makin' me choose, Bryce. And I don't like it."

"I'm sorry, Stodla. But he killed those two women. And he brought that gang down from Canada and got my brother killed because of it."

He went to the door, defeated and all, and then looked back at me and said: "Don't make me choose, Bryce. Please don't."

Right then, I felt sorry as hell for both of us. Sometimes

you wish you could just change your stance and make peace
but you can't because too much has happened. That's where
Stodla was and that's where I was.

I listened to him going down the stairs. He moved slow
and sad.

There was no funeral home wagon in front of the hospital.
A nurse sat on the steps, smoking a cigarette. This was the
height of brazen hussiness, a woman smoking in public.
But she'd likely been working long hours and didn't much
give a damn what folks thought about her tobacco habit.

Laura Westcott was in the six-bed ward, making late afternoon rounds. The first thing I noticed was that all six patients were sitting up. The previous patients had usually
been in a deep, sweaty sleep. These men looked sick but not
too sick. They seemed to have the affliction about as badly
as I had it.

The second thing I noticed was how the men watched
her. Schoolboy crushes. She was just that kind of woman.
There's something fascinating about good women. They
offer you a hope for humanity you don't always feel. Their
demeanor and behavior tells you that you can be better than
you thought you were, that life can have purpose and meaning, that you don't have to give in to your worst side. Of
course, it doesn't hurt if the woman is as good-looking as
Laura, or as playful as she was with her patients. She joked
and teased and laughed with them but somehow never lost
her dignity.

She was also very sharp medically. One kind of cough
told her one thing; another kind of cough told her something else. She picked up on the subtle distinctions instantly,
noting these on her chart and speaking aloud to her patient.

You could tell they didn't want her to leave. Six men in

bed all day slogging through a swampy fever and muscle aches so bad they made you want to cry—she was a shining example of all that was good and clean and pleasurable in life. Hell, who wouldn't want her to stay?

A few minutes later, I was walking down the hall with her.

"My Lord, I heard about Jenny Rice."

"Let's go to your office."

She glanced anxiously at me. "Is something wrong?"

"I don't want anyone else to hear us."

She nodded.

When we were seated, and the door was closed, I leaned forward and told her what had really happened out there the previous night.

"Jed didn't think any of this through very well," I said. "Too many people knew about him setting up the bank job and killing his brother."

"Why didn't he just kill Donald himself?"

"He did, but he couldn't let anybody know it. He'd be the chief suspect right away. He inherited the bank if Donald died. He inherited the Wylie family mantle if Donald died. He inherited the town influence if Donald died. Pekins would've gone right after him."

"So he talked Jenny into taking the fall."

"She was willing to risk a jury finding her innocent."

"But, Lord, why would she take a risk like that? She was hardly stupid."

"Jed's charm. She'd fallen in love with him. He'd set her up and seduced her into it. The trouble was, it all started to come undone. The bank gang was killed. And Susan Baxter decided she didn't trust him. Jenny had to be wondering if he really was going to leave his wife and run away with her, as he'd promised. Pekins and I took care of the bank gang for him. And then he took care of both Susan and Jenny in one fell swoop: a murder-suicide between two jealous women. Even Pekins went along with it at first."

"And now he believes your version?"

"If I can give him hard evidence."

"And how will you do that?"

I shook my head. "I need sleep first. A spell is coming on. And it's coming on early."

"That happen sometimes."

"After I sleep, I've got an idea of what I can do. But I need to think about it some more."

"Anything I can do, let me know. I mean that."

"I know you do."

"He killed Paul."

"Yes, he did." I just sat and looked at her, no less enchanted than the men in the ward had been. She represented all the things Paul wanted and deserved and all the things I wanted and would never have. And then, sitting there watching her like that, something changed in me. I was still enchanted but she became permanently fixed in my mind as Paul's. I saw the family they could have had together and the years they could've spent and the comfort and succor they could have given each other in a hundred different circumstances. She was Paul's. No matter what happened to her—whether she married or not—a part of her would always be Paul's.

"He loved you."

"He's all I think of."

"We're going to get Jed."

She pulled open the middle drawer of her desk, brought out a Navy Colt. "I know we are."

She was full of surprises. "You know how to use that damned thing?" I asked.

"My brother was a major in the Union army. He taught

me how to shoot. And when the time comes, that's just what I plan to do." Then she put the gun away. "I've tried getting it off my mind—Jed Wylie bringing them down here in the first place—but I can't." No tears now for Laura, just cold, considered rage. She wasn't the pretty schoolmarm anymore. The boys in the ward wouldn't have recognized her now. She was somebody else, somebody who looked fetching and familiar until you looked at the shadowed eyes. And then she was just a little bit scary.

"I need to get back to my rounds," she said.

I went back to my hotel room and slept.

TWENTY

I WASN'T SURE what time the fever came. I used the chamber pot twice to throw up. I was so cold at one point I piled all my clothes on top of the blankets. Then, when the fever came back, I was so hot I slept in nothing but my long johns.

When it was all done, I cleaned up my room, taking the chamber pot out to the alley and washing it out with water from the horse trough. It was embarrassing to leave a room like that.

When I went to the café, it was just suppertime. Couples filled the table; a few had brought rambunctious kids along. The couples could only eat between bouts with the little ones. I had Irish coffee. I couldn't decide which tasted better, the coffee or the whiskey. One cup gave me enough jitters and juice to wake me up completely from my spell with the fever.

I thought I might see Stodla here. By now, he had to

have realized that what I'd told him was true. He had to be able to see Jed for what he was, what he'd always been.

I was halfway through my meal when Pekins came in. He saw me, came over uninvited, and sat down.

"Guess who I just spent two hours with?"

"I'm not much for guessing, Chief."

"Your friend Jed."

"Oh?"

"He stopped by around three this afternoon. Said you'd told his friend Stodla a couple of whoppers about him."

"I see."

"The same whoppers you told me, as it turned out."

I finished up my pork chop. He occupied himself with his pipe.

"He has asked me to escort you out of town."

"And you're going to?"

"I told him I'd think about it." He kept the pipe tucked into the corner of his mouth as he spoke. "I also asked him where he happened to be at the time Jenny Rice was shooting the Baxter woman."

"Jed was always good with alibis."

"He's got a good one. Seems his littlest daughter is running a bad fever. And so is his wife. Not malaria, just an average case of influenza. Anyway, Jed claims that he spent most of the time between ten and two waiting on his wife and daughter. The gunshots were heard around eleven o'clock."

"So his wife is his alibi?"

He took his pipe from his mouth and smiled coldly. "Oh, no, that wouldn't be enough for Jed. He has to gild the lily—not only can his wife and seven-year-old daughter testify that he was home, so can the maid. She was there helping Jed with the wife and daughter."

"You talked to the maid?"

"I did."

"And she said—?"

"She said just what Jed said."

"And you believe her?"

He studied me a moment.

"I shouldn't like you, Lamont. But I do. Not a lot, but a little. And I shouldn't trust you. But I do. Not a lot, but a little"

"And that means?"

"It means there's something wrong with the whole setup. Jenny Rice killing the Baxter woman, I mean. I could see the possibility of Jenny feeling so hurt and so angry with Donald that she killed him. But I can't see her killing the Baxter woman. Why would she? Donald was already dead."

"So now you arrest Jed?"

The pipe went back into his mouth. "For what? He has a very solid alibi. He also has a great deal of prestige in this town, especially now that he runs the bank. So I'm to take your word over his? I'd be fired by the town council and replaced immediately."

"They're in his pocket?"

He smiled coldly again. "Proof, Mr. Lamont. Even if I believe you, you can't prove what you say and neither can I. Even if everything you say is true—that Jenny didn't actually kill Donald, he did; and that he brought the gang down from Canada; and that he killed the two women to keep them quiet—how the hell do we go about finding proof? The only person who knows the whole story is Jed. And I don't expect him to help us out anytime soon, do you?"

"So we just give up?"

"We give up unless you have the kind of dumb luck nobody ever has and stumble into some kind of proof."

"So he just walks the street a free man."

A laugh. "You sound very naïve for a man who served
time. The streets are filled with killers and you know it.
The prisons are filled with men who got railroaded in there.
And my sister is very likely married to a man who got away
with murder. It's not a perfect world, Mr. Lamont. In case
you hadn't noticed, I mean." He stood up, short, trim, dapper. "I'm a professional peace officer, Mr. Lamont. I even
have a sheepskin saying I graduated with honors from the
Milwaukee Police Academy. I'm very proud of that. And I
practice everything I learned in there. And one of those
things was to never bother the county attorney about a case
unless you've got proof enough to help him get a convic-
tion. That's where the proof comes in. And in this particular case, there's one more kicker."

"Oh?"

"The county attorney is Jed's first cousin."

I smiled. "You enjoyed telling me that, didn't you?"

"My mom always says I enjoy shocking people. And I
guess I do." Then he went to shake hands and shoot the
breeze with the people of the town who happened to be
dining here on this fine evening.

I didn't sleep well. I kept thinking about Jed. I played out
all kinds of fantasies in my mind. He died a hundred different ways. And he always died screaming.

I smoked a dozen cigarettes, enough to get me cough-
ing. I put a serious dent in a new pint of whiskey, too. I
ended up, near dawn, in the rocking chair and as I sat there
quietly rocking, I thought of Susan Baxter and her diary
and how sad it was that she never was able to find peace

before she died. I leaned forward, remembering the night in the gazebo with Jenny Rice. The night she mentioned her journal.

I wondered if Pekins had found it. But no, if he had he would've said something.

There would be the proof. If she kept the journal dutifully at all there'd be a lot in it about how she'd been captivated by Jed. She might not have put it all in there—the whole plan he'd concocted—but surely there'd be references to Jed that would establish their connection.

I slept till nine, got up, ordered hot water for the bathtub, and got myself all shined up for the day. If I was tired from lack of sleep, I wasn't going to admit it. Especially not to myself.

After breakfast, I went out to the Rice house. Moonlight and shadow had given it an opulence that daylight took away. The roof needed repair; some of the trim paint was peeling; the lawn needed a good raking and seeding.

I knocked. It was some time before Fogarty showed up.

"Oh," he said, seeing who it was.

"I thought your wife would answer."

He made a face. "She had to go to Daly City for a while. Her sister took sick. Good thing she wasn't around the other night with what-all happened."

I said, "If you'll open the screen door, Fogarty, I'll give you ten dollars."

"You will?"

"Yes."

"And that's all I have to do? Just open the door?"

"That's all you have to do if all you want is ten dollars."

"And if I want more?"

"That's where we start to bargain."

He smiled. "You're so full of shit."

I smiled back. "Yeah, I am kinda, aren't I?"

"What you want? The bitch is dead."

"How'd you put up with her?"

His old black face looked sad. "I got the cancer. Had it now for six years. Woulda left but I wanted to stay close to my doc—only colored doc in the whole area—and this was the only job I could find, man my age and my color'n all."

He pushed the door open and walked outside. He wore a faded shirt, ratty sweater, and house slippers that slapped and flapped when he walked. He inhaled deeply of the serene, sweet day.

"I always figure if I could live to be old enough, it wouldn't bother me to die. Man, I don't think *nobody* ever lives to be that old. I'z still scared of it."

"Me, too."

"I just don't want to be no sissy is all. I seen men die and they's cryin' and wailin' and carryin' on like sissies. I seen my old man die like that, so scared and all. He was jes' beggin' to stay alive. I sure hope they shoot me before I do somethin' like that."

"The animals have the right idea."

"That's right. Just crawl away and die somewheres all by yourself." He narrowed his eyes. "How come you're out here, anyway?"

"Looking for something."

"Lookin' for what?"

"You know what a diary is?"

"If this wasn't such a fine day—and I wasn't in such a fine mood because the bitch is dead—I'd tell you where to shove it. You think jes' because I'm colored and all I don't know what a fuckin' diary is?"

He was right. I had sounded like I was talking to a seven-year-old. "You know where she kept hers?"

He shook his head. "They fixed it up—her lawyer did—so I could stay here for a long while. And that's jes' what I plan to do. And I sure don't want to buy into no white-man trouble."

"I just want her journal."

"Oh, sure, and then you'll want somethin' else and then you'll want somethin' else. And then I'll be right in the middle of it. And you know who always gits in the worst trouble of all? A colored man like me. Because nobody ever gives a shit what happens to him. He die and they just pitch him in a shallow grave, no better'n a squirrel or somethin' like that. Well, that ain't happenin' to me, I'll tell you that. You take your white-man trouble and you keep it."

"Don't you want to know who killed her?"

"Far as I'm concerned, she killed herself."

"I think you know better than that."

"I don't know jack shit and I plan to keep it that way. The white man never done jack for me except rape my sisters and beat my pa. I come up on a plantation and I sure don't forget what I seen there, either. Colored men stick to colored problems and white men stick to white-man problems and that's the way it should be."

"What if I gave you fifty dollars?"

"That's just askin' for white men to come around and give me trouble. I don't know what's in that book of hers but I'd bet Yankee money it's stuff she didn't want nobody to know about. And that means trouble."

A whistle sounded. "My tea," he said. "Better tend to it."

"Fogarty," I said, taking his sleeve. "I really need that book."

"Hell, I'm just a dumb colored man. You didn't even

think I knew what a diary was, remember?" He smiled at me. He took a lot of pleasure in mocking me the way I'd unintentionally mocked him. "Jes' a pore ol' cotton-head, tha's me, boss." He went back inside.

I was walking back to town when Laura Westcott pulled up in a buggy. She offered me a ride and I took it.

"You're going to hear about it."

"Hear about what?"

"What I did to Jed Wylie about an hour ago."

"Oh, and what was that?"

"Slapped him. Couldn't control myself. We were both in the general store and he was being his usual self—you know how he likes to act like the boss politician—and I just couldn't deal with it right then. So right in front of everybody, I slapped him."

"Hard?"

"Hard enough to draw blood."

The houses got smaller, closer together as we drew near the business district.

"What'd *he* do?"

"Pretended to be very understanding. He was lying to all the ladies in the store. Said I'd been through a lot with Paul dying and putting in all the long hours with the malaria outbreak and he could certainly understand how I'd just naturally take it out on somebody. I think the women would have elected him governor on the spot. They flocked right to him. You should've heard them telling him how gentle and understanding and kind a man he was, and they just wished that their husbands could be more like him. Most people don't see him for what he is, do they?"

"No. No, they don't."

"And so anything *we* do we have to do on our own."

I thought of the gun she'd pulled from her drawer earlier in the day. "I loved Paul, too, don't forget," I reminded her. "And one way or another, I'm going to make Jed pay. But the worst thing either one of us could do right now is force any kind of showdown. We need evidence. And it may take longer to get than we want it to. But we'll just mess up everything if we move too fast or do something rash. You understand?"

"I hate him."

"I know you do."

"I want him to pay." She was cold again, a stranger, and a scary one.

"He *will* pay, Laura. We just have to have a little patience."

She glanced over at me. "I can't eat, I can't sleep. I even started smoking cigarettes again. He's all I can think of. It's funny. I don't even think of Paul that much anymore. There's no room in my mind for anybody except Jed Wylie."

"We'll get him."

As we pulled onto Main Street, she said, "We'd better."

I rested for two hours. Didn't really sleep, couldn't. Just closed my eyes and lay there. Maybe Fogarty didn't even *know* where the diary was. Maybe he'd just been teasing the white man.

A headache came and went. While it lasted, it felt as if my head were being stepped on by a very large animal.

I thought about Laura. I'd always be attracted to her, couldn't help it. But I saw now that she was more entangled in Paul's death than even I was. She would take a long, long time getting over it. And maybe she never *would* get over it. There was no point in telling her how I felt, no point at all.

After one hour, I got up and got myself a drink of water. And I collapsed right back on the bed, my legs gone entirely. I cleared my mind as well as I could and lay there with my eyes closed.

The knock was gentle. I wondered if I'd have the strength to answer it. Finally, I got up from bed. I felt stronger than I would've thought.

I went to the door. Mrs. Grayson stood there. "I'd appreciate it if you'd let me talk to you."

I'd never heard her so polite. "All right."

She came in. "I know this isn't the thing a proper woman would do, calling on a stranger in his hotel room."

"I don't think you have anything to worry about, Mrs. Grayson."

"I worry about appearances, Mr. Lamont. Appearances matter as much as fact. Maybe even more, in some instances."

"I don't suppose you'd want whiskey or a cigarette?"

"I think you know better than that."

"Then please indulge a sinner. Because I'm about to have both."

She wore a cute little hat and white gloves and a dressy gingham dress. Despite her age, she was not without her charms. She'd been born cute and would die cute, no matter how many years her tombstone logged.

She said, "He broke his arm."

"Who broke whose arm?"

"Jed broke my husband's arm."

"I see. Any idea why?"

"My husband went to see Chief Pekins. Pekins wasn't there but Stodla saw him go into the chief's office and told Jed. Jed paid us a visit late last night. He intentionally broke my husband's arm."

"What's your husband got on Jed?"

She cleared her throat. "If he tells, he goes to prison,

too. That's why I didn't want him to tell. But he went to see Pekins anyway."

"Your husband have anything to do with the robbery?"

"Of course not."

"He knew Jed was embezzling money from the bank while Donald was still alive, didn't he? What'd Jed do, pay him off so he couldn't talk?" I already knew the answer to that—Stodla had told me. But I wanted to know how much she would let on.

She shook her head. "I'm not saying any more."

"Why did you come here?"

"I thought maybe you could talk to Jed."

I laughed. "You haven't kept up, Mrs. Grayson. Jed would kill me now the first chance he got."

"But why?"

"Because I know things about him even your husband doesn't know. He wants to have himself a nice, easy life here. He can't do that with your husband and me still hanging around. We're too much of a threat to him."

"Then you think my husband *should* go to Pekins?"

"Not right away. The only thing that would prove is that Jed embezzled some money," I said. "There are a lot more serious charges out there. Those are the ones I'm interested in. In the meantime, tell your husband to just wait till he hears from me."

For the first time, she smiled. She appreciated the respite my words had given her.

"No Pekins, then?"

"Not for right now," I assured her.

"I can't tell you how much I appreciate this." She went to the door, then paused and turned to me. "I love my husband very much."

"I'm sure you do."

She was still smiling. "I'll tell him what you said, Mr. Lamont. Thank you so much."

Later, I twice walked past the Rice estate. The windows were shuttered, the doors closed. Fogarty was in hiding, if he was even there.

The second time I walked past, I decided to check the wrought-iron front gate. But just as I stepped forward, a neighbor passed by and gave me a long, suspicious look.

I walked back to my room and took a short nap. When I got up, the sweat started sluicing down my body. At least the fever had broken.

I had dinner and a cigar and some brandy. I stopped by the hospital, but I didn't bother Laura. She looked too busy.

For two hours I sat in a poker game. I came out about even. I was walking back to my hotel room when I decided I'd give the Rice place one more try.

Climbing over the back section of iron fence took most of my strength. For several long minutes after, I lay on the grass, letting the exertion carry me into a kind of semi-slumber.

No watchdogs that I could hear or see. No Pinkertons walking the perimeters.

Of course, getting over the fence would be the easy part. Getting inside would be the trick. And then finding the damned thing.

When I felt strong enough, I got to my feet and started toward the vast house silhouetted against the full moon. Gray rain clouds scudded past.

I didn't see him. A black man, he was one more shadow in a night of shadows. He came from nowhere. Holding a Colt on me.

"I was looking for you, Fogarty."

"My ass. You was looking for the diary."

"Same thing, I suppose. Being that you've got it."

"Damned right I got it. She used to write in it every day up in the attic room she fixed up for herself. Always saw where she put it away, too."

"You read it?"

"Read it every day. Always good for a laugh. Stupid, spoiled bitch. Thought she was Cleopatra or somebody like that."

"You have it now?"

"Sure, I have it."

"How much you want for it?"

" 'Fraid I can't help you there, Lamont. Ole Jed Wylie already tol' me he'd pay top dollar for it."

Wylie knew it would probably be in her diary, all of it from the embezzlement to the robbery.

"Maybe I can top his offer."

"Not likely, Lamont. Sorry. You ask me which man I like better, you or ole Jed, and I'd take you any day. But this is my ticket out of here. And I need to take all the money I can."

"How'd he find out you had the book?"

"I saw Stodla overtown. Tol' him to tell Wylie. Stodla came by less'n a half hour later. Ole Jed, he really wants this book."

"I'll bet he does."

We'd talked long enough here in the chilling darkness for Fogarty to relax a little too much. He wasn't prepared for me to pull my .45 from my waistband.

"Give it to me," I said. "Pekins needs it."

"Pekins can piss up a rope for all I care."

"C'mon, Fogarty. Hand it over."

"Yeah, Fogarty," said a voice behind me. "C'mon. Hand it over." There was a pleasant wry tone in his mocking.

He'd always been good at mimicking people. And he'd had a lot of practice over the years with me.

For a man his size, he'd always been able to move well, too, silently.

He'd managed, in the gloom and my preoccupation with Fogarty, to get within a few feet of me. Now he was right in back of me. The barrel of his pistol jabbed the back of my head.

"I want you to give Stodla your gun, Bryce," he said. "Just for old times' sake."

Stodla came around from behind me.

"I sure wish you'd left town like I told you, Bryce," he said, taking my gun and handing it over butt first to Jed.

My eyes had adjusted to the moon-washed darkness.

Fogarty said, "You bring the money?"

Jed said, "I've got it right here, Mr. Fogarty. You bring the book?"

"I've got it right here," Fogarty said, and patted an area near his ribs.

I just hope for your sake this is all you say it is, Mr. Fogarty. I'd be very unhappy if you oversold it to me."

"Well, all you do, Mr. Wylie, is you read the first few pages and you'll see why you wouldn't want no snoopy lawman like Pekins to see this. She never kept a diary until you and her started goin' around together. Practically this whole thing is about you."

Jed laughed. "I hope she extolled my manly virtues in the boudoir."

"She sure did that," Fogarty said. "She sure did that."

"You think you'll be able to kill me?" I asked Stodla.

"What're you talkin' about, Bryce?"

"Don't pay any attention to him. You know how he likes to start trouble among people. That's why he was always such a bad gang member. Too much of a troublemaker. He always has to do things his way."

"He won't kill me. No guts. So he'll make you kill me. Just the way he made you kill Donald."

It was a guess but a lucky one.

"He said he couldn't do it, Donald bein' his brother and all."

"You think you can shoot me, Stodla?"

"Aw, don't go and talk like that, Bryce. He told me he was gonna let you go soon as he got the book."

"Well, he's just about got the book. Let's see if he lets me go."

Jed said, "Let's make the exchange, shall we, Mr. Fogarty?" He reached inside his suit jacket and took out a long white envelope. It looked thick and heavy.

"I believe this is yours, Mr. Fogarty," he said, handing over the envelope with a bit of ceremony. "And I believe the diary is mine."

Fogarty spoiled the moment by having to wrestle the diary from where he had it stuck inside his shirt.

Jed took it and put it in his jacket pocket. It was a small, leather-bound blue book with a gold lock. He made a point of not opening it, just slipped it in there.

I said, "So where're you going to have Stodla kill me?"

"Right here," Jed said. "You and Mr. Fogarty here got into some kind of argument and you each killed the other in a gunfight."

And with that, he took a pistol from his holster and shot Fogarty dead on in the heart. He put two more bullets in him quickly.

Fogarty died slumping to the ground and holding his chest. He looked genuinely surprised. He shouldn't have been. This was Jed.

Then Jed reached in his pocket and took out a smaller Colt. "And this is the gun Mr. Fogarty used on you."

He'd had this all worked out in advance. Nobody had ever accused Jed of being dumb.

"So long, Bryce."

"No! You can't kill him, Jed! This is Bryce! We rode together all those years!" Stodla came out of the shadows.

Jed looked irritated. "Dammit, Frank. If I'd asked *you* to kill him, you'd have bitched that you couldn't do it. So now I decided to do you a favor and do it myself, and you're still bitching about it. Now just stand back."

"I won't let you kill him, Jed. Not Bryce."

I wasn't sure exactly what happened then. It was just dark enough for their motions to be obscured in shadow. The only thing I knew for sure was that a few moments later—following the exchange of four or five bullets—Frank Stodla pitched forward, groaning.

"Fuck," Jed said. "Believe it or not, I didn't want to do that."

Stodla's legs jerked and spasmed and he threw up blood. At least it looked sort of like blood, the fluid leaking from his mouth and all down his chin.

Disbelief. Rage. Frank Stodla didn't deserve this kind of death for standing up to Jed for the first time in his life.

"Yeah, well, you did it, Jed. You fucking killed him."

"I actually liked ole Frank."

"Yeah, and you showed it, too." My voice dripped with sarcasm. "You treated him so well."

He held his gun on me. He was looking at Stodla. And then he shifted his gaze to me.

"I never liked you, Bryce."

"I never liked you, either."

"You always thought you were better than the rest of us."

"Maybe I was. You ever think of that?"

"And," he said, "you were always a smart-mouthed prick. Just like you are now."

"Shoot me, Jed. Don't talk me to death."

He smiled. "You tryin' to tell me you're not scared?"

"I'd rather die than have to listen to you gloat, Jed. I mean, if those are my only choices." I lunged then. I didn't have any choice. And I lunged for a lot of reasons: for what he'd done to my kid brother, for what he'd done to Stodla, for what he'd done to Sally or Susan Baxter, for what he'd done to Fogarty.

And for not giving one good damn that I got sent to prison for a job that he'd messed up.

"You bastard!"

He tried to fight me but he'd lost sight of me momentarily in the shadows. He fired two quick shots. One hit but it didn't seem to bother me much and the other missed entirely.

He was stronger than me and maybe even a little bit quicker, but I think I hated him more than he hated me, so after what seemed like ten minutes of beating the shit out of each other, I'd inflicted slightly more damage. I got two black eyes; he got a broken nose. I kneed him hard enough in the groin so that he was bowlegged when I finally yanked him to his feet. Then I couldn't resist one last indignity: I kicked him so hard in the kneecap that he fell over face-down and lay there sobbing.

It wasn't easy getting him back to town.

TWENTY-ONE

"**M**AYBE I OUGHT to hire you, Lamont," Pekins said when I brought Jed in.

"I don't think I'd make much of a lawman."

He laughed. "Actually, neither do I."

Jed Wylie wanted a lawyer. Jed Wylie wanted a cell of his own. Jed Wylie wanted the diary back I'd stolen from him. Jed Wylie wanted his brother-in-law to arrest me for trespassing on Jenny Rice's property.

He was all sputter and splutter, Jed was, a powerful man who was suddenly left with his pockets turned out and bare. No power at all.

While Pekins took him back to the cell, I found a small, empty office and sat there with a cup of coffee I'd cadged and read through the diary.

When Pekins came in, he said, "Learn anything?"

"I know where the rest of the robbery money is."

"Where?"

"In the bank."

"No shit?"

"It never left there, according to the diary. Jed took it down in the basement the night before the robbery. Put it in a safe down there. The gang only took half."

"I'll be damned."

"I think he figured that when he put the reward on their heads, he'd get the rest of the money, and the gang members weren't gonna come out of this alive anyway, so he'd have it back, plus some insurance money for what was still allegedly missing."

"He's a smart sonofabitch, I've got to give him that."

"You'd better get your mortuary man out to Jenny Rice's place." I told him about Fogarty and Stodla.

"Poor old Fogarty. He was always waiting for his ship to come in." Then, "So what happens to you?"

"I leave town in the morning. Get a good night's sleep first."

"How's the malaria?"

"Getting a little better. One day at a time, the doc said."

"She's quite a lady."

"Yeah. My brother sure seemed to think so, anyway."

"Sorry about him, Lamont. You know I thought well of him."

I put my hand out and we shook. "I never thought I'd say this to a lawman, Pekins, but I actually like you a little bit."

"Same for me. Never thought I'd care for a crook. But you're about the most decent crook I ever met."

I smiled. "You'd still arrest me if I ran a game here, though."

He laughed. "Hell, yes, I would. That's my part of the game."

The café was closed, so instead I went to the least noisy

of the saloons. The three men at the bar were already talking about Jed. Nothing like the fa'l of an important man to
take over the conversation.

The two beers I had didn't set well. I went back out into
the cool night air. And then my arm started stinging. The
wound was so minor, I'd forgotten it. There wasn't even
much blood. But for some reason now it was getting un-
comfortable.

I went over to the hospital and asked for Laura. I figured she'd be gone, this late and all, and she was.

A young man who reminded me a little of Paul fixed
me up. "You got off lucky."

"I sure did."

He did his work quickly and well. I gave him two dollars and was on my way. I walked to my hotel and slowly
climbed the stairs to my room.

I was just letting myself in when the man next door, all
muttonchop sideburns and rum-blazed eyes, said, "The
pretty gal was lookin' for you."

"The doctor?"

"Yeah, that's right. The doctor."

"When was this?"

"Oh, 'bout an hour or so ago, I guess."

"She leave any kind of message?"

"Just said she'd see you tomorrow is all."

"Thanks."

Before I got to sleep, I wondered what Laura had wanted.
Probably to celebrate nailing Jed. It would be over for her
now and after the proper time of mourning, she could get
on with her life. There was no sense in her wasting it on
mourning forever. It's nice when people make claims like
that—like I'll never want anybody else now that he's dead.
But they rarely stick to it. The man or woman who says

that usually gets himself hitched again in six months or so. I hoped it would happen for Laura like that.

I slept.

This night's dream was about the farm back in Pennsylvania. Mom and Dad were still alive. Paul was trailing after me. We were looking for spring mushrooms. Mom always sent us looking for them. It didn't have any particular ending, the dream. It was just a nice day and we were having a nice time was all.

I woke up and was sick to my stomach, but not much. I really was getting better. When I lay down again, I could feel the fever. It was like the surface of my skin was on fire, but it was faint this time.

I drifted off. Paul and Laura were getting married. I must've been best man. I was standing on the altar with them. Pekins was there. And Susan Baxter. And Mom and Dad. It was a pretty strange dream, all those dead people alive again, but it was a pleasant dream because Paul and Laura were so happy. She was beautiful, of course, and every little boy in the church got a crush on her.

I'm not sure how long it took him to wake me up.

My memory is that I didn't *want* to wake up and he really had to shake me hard and yell directly into my ear. And then I was awake and sitting up.

". . . maybe she'll listen to you, Lamont," Pekins was saying. "That's why you need to go get her."

It was dawn in the window. But I didn't know what he was talking about. That she'd listen to me? And that's why *I* was the one who needed to go get her? Who was *she?* And why would she listen to me? And why did I need to go get her?

He found my pint and he found my cigarettes and he put them in my hands and I did the right thing by them.

The whiskey burned my belly. The cigarette turned the crank on my heart.

"Now say it again," I said. "Slow. I was really out."

"No shit, you were really out. I thought you were dead."

"Gee, I'm sorry I have this malaria, Chief. You know I got it just so I could piss you off."

"All right, all right. Don't get pissy with me. You need to listen and listen good."

"Then tell me."

"She shot him."

"Who shot him?"

"Laura Westcott."

"Shot who?"

"Jed Wylie."

"Oh, shit."

"That's right. Walked into my office about two hours ago, put something in the night officer's coffee, and when he was unconscious, she went into the four cells we've got and shot him. Point blank. Right in front of about six, seven witnesses who were in the cells. Didn't say a word to him, either. Then just turned around and walked out the door."

I thought of the gun she'd taken from her desk. I thought of her stopping by my room to talk to me. And me not being there.

"Is he dead?"

"Not quite. But he's not going to make it. She put four bullets in his chest."

"Fuck."

"Yeah."

"Where is she?"

"You know that property she and your brother were going to buy?"

"Yeah."

"That's where she is. Holed up in that little shack they were going to tear down."

"You got men there?"

"Yeah. I told them not to do anything till I get back. My sense of things is she'll kill herself if we try and rush her."

"So I go and talk to her."

"That's the idea."

"What if she won't talk to me?"

"Then at least we'll have tried."

"Shit," I said.

I was groggy and cranky. I needed to piss; I had a headache; and at the moment, I was freezing. I took care of as many of my dilemmas as I could and then tugged on my clothes.

When we got outside, the town was just starting to come alive for the day. There was wagon traffic in the street already and the swamper from one of the saloons was sweeping off the front steps. The Catholic church would soon ring its bell for six o'clock mass.

Pekins had a wagon waiting. As we were climbing aboard, another cop walked briskly down the street.

"Just came from the hospital, Chief," he said.

"Yeah?" Pekins said.

"Jed Wylie," the cop said, "he died about five minutes ago."

TWENTY-TWO

THERE WAS A crowd.

There would be, of course.

Who could resist the possibility of seeing even more violence? Especially when it involved a pretty woman who had the stature of a doctor?

There were probably twenty, thirty of them, and they looked eager as kids at a circus. There were three buckboards and six or seven men in khaki uniforms and a number of shotguns. Everything was somber and official.

Pekins's men kept them back on the dusty road. The shack stood maybe fifteen yards into the tall-grass plot of land.

There was no sign of trouble. The old wood shack still provided a perch for crows and blackbirds. The creek behind it was still packed with noisy frogs. A breeze from the west pitched the wildflowers into a kind of dance.

No indication that a woman who'd just murdered somebody was inside the shack.

Pekins said, as we drew up to his men, "She say anything?"

They shook their heads.

Pekins pulled the wagon to a stop and we jumped down.

"You have a gun?" he said.

"I seem to have lost it in all the trouble last night."

He waved for one of his officers to come over.

"Yes, sir?" The kid looked snappy in his khaki uniform.

"Give him your gun."

"What, sir?"

"I said give him your gun."

"Sir, you said the first thing a lawman had to learn was never to give up his gun."

Pekins looked at me. Rolled his eyes. "I trained them too well." Then, "Now, give him your gun."

"Yes, sir." The kid reluctantly handed his weapon over to me.

"Now get the hell back there with Stenvig."

"Yes, sir."

It was a standard-issue Colt .45.

"Anything in particular you want me to do with this?" I said.

"Yeah. I want you to throw it on the ground."

"You want me to do what?"

"You need it as a prop."

"I wish I knew what the hell you were talking about."

He squinted at me in the hard prairie sunlight. "In a minute or so, Lamont, I'm going up to the edge of that plot of land and yell to her I'm sending you in. You with me so far?"

"I think I can handle that."

"Then, to show her we don't have anything tricky in

mind, you take out the gun I just got you and you drop it on the ground."

"I see."

"Then you go in and just hope she doesn't shoot you."

"I don't think she'll shoot me."

"I don't think she will, either, Lamont. If I did, I wouldn't ask you to go in there." Then, "You ready?"

"Ready."

"Push those people back," he said to his officers.

He walked across the dusty road. He climbed a ways into the tall grass. Cupped his hand to his mouth.

"Laura? I'm sending Lamont in. He wants to talk to you. He's your friend. I think you know that."

There was no response.

"Laura, can you hear me?" The breeze was his only answer. He turned around and looked at me. "Now, you walk up to about where I am and throw your gun down. Got it?"

He was treating me with the same impatience and condescension he did his troops. Any other time, it would have made me smile.

"Got it, Chief," I said.

"Then get up here."

I walked up to him. He faded back to the road. I lifted my gun up to where she could easily see it and said in a loud voice, "Laura, I'm pitching my gun. I'm coming in unarmed."

I held the weapon up as high as I could, barely keeping it aloft with the tips of my fingers. Then I flung it as far as I could. It disappeared in the tall grass. "I want to talk to you, Laura." I started moving.

The old shack had one window. No glass in it. A stretch of ragged cotton shirt had been nailed across it. I could see a vague shadow moving behind the cotton. Laura. With her gun, no doubt.

None of it was very dramatic.

I suppose the crowd was hoping for something memorable enough to keep talking about for weeks and months afterwards. But it rarely is dramatic, not if you stick to the facts. I've seen lawmen bring in, and bring down, any number of seminotorious gunnies and what's always amazed me is how dull it usually is. The gunnies are always pretty much outnumbered, the lawman in charge isn't there to give a speech on law and order—he just wants to get his ass back to town in one piece so he can see his grandkids in the coming years—and the gunny doesn't want to give any of the deputies any reason to kill him, which he knows they're just itching to do. So the whole thing is about as eventful as buying some hard candy at a general store: Here's your money, my man; and here's your candy, Sheriff. It's about as dramatic as that.

She didn't call out for me to stay back. She didn't take a shot at me. She didn't even *threaten* to take a shot at me.

I just walked up to the shack. The door was warped as hell and stubborn. It took me a couple of good lunges to get it open. Then I went inside: table, two chairs, two shelves for canned goods. All slimy and rotten with age.

A lot of prairie animals had seen fit to use this as both an outhouse and a burial ground. The stench was ungodly. I made a face.

"God, this smells."

"You get used to it. Be in a room with ten men with malaria sometime."

She sat on a dingy box in the corner. Her Navy Colt sat on the floor in front of her. She said, "I'm not sorry I did it."

"God, I wish you would've talked to me."

"I was thinking about what you said, about my life going on and everything. And you were wrong. There never would've been anybody else for me except Paul. It's just the kind of woman I am. I can't help it any more than you can help having blue eyes."

"The state would've hanged him for you."

She shook her head. She looked exhausted and slightly crazed. "Wouldn't have been the same. Had to be personal. I had to see his fear. It didn't last long. I had to shoot him right away and get out of there. But it was long enough. He begged me. And that was all I wanted. I *wanted* him to beg me. I wanted to see him lose his arrogance. And he did."

"Pekins would like you to just give yourself up."

She shook her head again. Even with her hair wild, her Gibson girl outfit dusty and dirty, and even with her face crazy and forlorn, she didn't lose that prairie beauty of hers, that hard dignity you see in the faces of pioneer women. She said, "Tell him I'm thinking about it. But I need a little more time. Alone."

"I think he'd like me to stay here with you."

"No offense. But I really do want to be alone."

I sighed. "You're all right?"

She nodded. "For somebody who's just killed a man, I'm fine."

"And you're not going to hurt yourself?"

"Hadn't even crossed my mind."

"Really?"

"Really."

"Then you won't mind if I take that gun?"

She leaned forward, picked it up, held it out for me.

I took it, slid it between my belly and belt. "There are a lot of things a good lawyer can do," I said.

"Yes. I agree."

"You might not have to serve much time."

"I've thought of that."

"I'll help you find a good one."

"I appreciate that, Bryce. Now I'd like to be here alone."

"Sure." I felt a lot better, having her gun and all. "Pekins'll be happy. He likes you."

"I like him, too. He's a good, honest man."

I went to the door.

She stood up. "I'll help you with that. It's easier to push it closed from inside."

She came over to me. I took her by the elbow and kissed her on the cheek. "I'm sorry all this happened to you."

She came into my arms then and held me with a little girl's desperation. The urgency of her embrace was so intense that it was a little bit frightening.

When we pulled apart, she said, "You're a good man, too. Thanks for everything, Bryce."

I walked outside. Waved to Pekins that everything was all right. He waved back.

Behind me, I heard her having trouble with the door. So warped, it was hard to close on the spring-swelled earthen floor. But when I turned around to help her with the door, I saw in one tiny terrible moment a six-gun come from somewhere in the folds of her skirt.

Then she was behind the door and I couldn't see anything.

But I could hear it. Just the one shot.

I shouted her name—at least I think I did—rammed myself against the door. It swung back completely.

She was sprawled backward on the floor. The other .45

had simply fallen from her hand. Now it rested on the ground next to her knee.

The hole in her temple was pretty big. The blood hadn't started to gush yet. The tight-packed air smelled of gunpowder.

Shouts came from the road. Somebody was running fast and flat-footed toward the shack. That would be Pekins.

No movement. I looked her over, head to toe. I took her pulse at three different body points and nothing. I put my head to her chest; my ear under her nose. Nothing, nothing, nothing. She was most certainly dead.

Peeking around the doorway, Pekins said, "Fuck. That's what I was afraid she'd do."

I stood up, my knees cracking. "I should've known."

"Oh, bullshit, Lamont. You couldn't have stopped her anyway. If she hadn't done it here she would've hanged herself in her cell. Or made a knife out of a spoon and cut her throat. She wanted to die and she did."

"Fuck," I said, just as he had.

"I'll get the mortuary people in here. They'll take good care of her. C'mon. I've got a pint we can split on the way back to town."

We didn't stop with his pint. When that was drained, we picked a saloon and spent the next three hours there. What we were doing was killing time till my train came.

"So where're you heading?"

"I'm not sure."

"Think you'll go straight?"

"What do you think?"

He smiled. "Probably not."

"Yeah," I said. "That's probably the safest answer. Probably not."

He had to get home to help his wife comfort his sister now that she was a widow—so I went to the depot alone.

My train was four hours late. By the time I got on board, I was sober again. And that was one thing I didn't want to be—sober—not for a long, long time.